Midnight in the Holy

City

Jared Bardon

Midnight in the Holy City

Contents

Chapter 1

The soldier's lifeless body was lying in a pool of blood. The flies had already begun to circle and land on the corpse, adding to its already disturbing appearance, but the sight of another dead comrade didn't bother Captain Thomas Altman. He had seen plenty of death since the War Between the States began. He was, however, curious as to why this soldier had met such a gruesome end. After all, the boy was only a courier— nobody important enough to murder. He knew the common criminals who roved the city usually steered clear of the military personnel. Most of them knew better than to try a man who had been trained to kill.

"Who found him?" Thomas asked the police constable.

"Two children, sir," the constable replied in a thick Irish accent. "They alerted me while I was walking to the station."

Thomas went down on his one good knee to examine the body. He recognized the soldier as a courier of General Ripley's but wasn't familiar with his name. He rolled the body over to find his victim died of a stab wound to the stomach. He also saw marks on the neck, indicating he was choked in the process of the murder, probably to muffle his screams. His eyes then diverted to the soldier's open brown carrying case. The markings "C.S.A." were engraved on a brass plate fastened to the front. It was suspiciously empty. He knew if the courier was on his way to deliver correspondence, the documents were now in the possession of someone else.

"Has your Detective Bureau been notified?" Thomas asked.

"Yes sir," the constable replied, taking off his uniform cap to wipe the sweat from his brow. The older, red-faced officer seemed extremely uncomfortable in the mid-day heat.

"There's no need to summon them now. We'll look after this one since he's military."

The officer didn't object. "Yes sir. I'll be on my way to let them know."

The July climate in Charleston, South Carolina made all the uniformed men feel extremely miserable. Thomas knew the constable was more than happy to leave.

Thomas stood up and motioned for his aide, Lieutenant Hudson Chase, who had been waiting nearby. Chase was frequently with him while the two were on duty and had proven to be an asset on past investigations.

"Sir?" Chase asked.

"Go and fetch a couple soldiers, the first ones you see. I'll also need you to bring a wagon. We need a way to get the body out of here. Take it to our headquarters when it's loaded so the colonel can have a look."

The young lieutenant saluted before running off toward King Street, the main thoroughfare in town.

Thomas took a moment to look at his surroundings. He could tell the courier was intentionally dumped in this alley to be out of sight for as long as possible, which wasn't normal for a simple robbery. It would have been easier to have left the boy where he fell.

The sound of men coming up the alley broke his concentration. Two young privates were heading his way, muskets resting on their shoulders. They were breathing heavily. Thomas thought Chase must have ordered them here on the double quick.

"The lieutenant told us to come to you, sir," one of the dirty-faced, gray-clad soldiers advised.

"Very good," he replied. "I need you men to stand here while we get the body moved. Wait until Lieutenant Chase comes back with the wagon."

"Yes sir," both soldiers replied in unison.

He took out a piece of paper from his jacket pocket and scribbled down a few notes: location of the body, manner of death, and the time the body was found. Once completed, he put the paper back in his pocket and left for his office.

As he made the walk, Thomas noticed several businesses boarded up that he hadn't noticed before. He was becoming increasingly disappointed at what his hometown had become. The war had turned the once vibrant city into a dreary place. Most of the shops, once busy selling wares from overseas, were now gone, forced out of business by the Yankee blockade of the harbor. The city's residents were also looking thinner. The Confederate government was rationing food to ensure the soldiers fighting the enemy stayed fed.

He arrived at the provost marshal's headquarters on Meeting Street. It was an old hotel, hastily converted into a military building after the fall of Fort Sumter. Consisting of two floors, the façade was accented by a large wraparound porch on the bottom story. Thomas had always thought the structure was too nice to be used as a government building, but the war had changed everything. The military was having to make use of all available resources. He saluted a sentry standing guard in the foyer before seeing his commanding officer, Colonel John Marlow, walking in his direction. Thomas didn't like him. He found his superior to be a brash and arrogant man, who never admitted he was wrong. To make matters worse, he had no formal military training. It was common knowledge that the colonel was appointed to his rank because of his wealth before the war. He had grown rich owning several rice plantations on the Cooper River just north of the city.

"Good morning, sir," Thomas greeted.

"Good morning," the colonel replied, putting on his hat and gloves. "Who was the man in the alley?"

"I believe the soldier was one of General Ripley's couriers, sir. I have seen him before but don't know his name."

The colonel looked concerned at the news. "Was he delivering any orders when he was killed?"

"I think so, sir. I found his case empty upon inspection."

"Make this a priority of the highest importance, Captain," the colonel ordered, pointing a forceful finger at Thomas. "We want to make sure the general stays abreast of our findings."

The colonel didn't wait for a reply. He moved rapidly out of the building and into the street.

Thomas already knew this was serious; he didn't need to be told that. The courier could have been delivering important orders, which in the hands of someone else, could be detrimental to the army. But these types of serious matters were his duties, and he performed his duties well. Thomas was assigned as the lead investigator in the office of the provost marshal for a reason—he was good at his job.

The sound of a wagon stopping in front of the building grabbed his attention. He looked to see Lieutenant Chase climbing off the buckboard. Thomas walked back outside to meet his aide.

"The colonel just left, Chase. It was a waste of time bringing him here," Thomas said, while peering at the courier's partially-covered body.

Chase shrugged. "What should we do with the body now, sir?"

Thomas wished he could tell the lieutenant to take the body to a mortician, but he knew the family of a lowly private didn't have the money to pay for embalming. "Take it to the pits north of town and give it to the diggers."

"Yes sir. I'll be back shortly," Chase answered before climbing back on the wagon and ordering the private at the reigns to drive away.

Thomas knew the burial ground north of town well. The large of number of soldiers dying from wounds and disease made the place quite busy.

Stepping back inside, he walked down the hallway and into his small white-walled office. He pulled the rickety chair from under the oak desk and sat down. Happy to be off his feet for a moment, Thomas rubbed his knee, hoping the achiness would ease. He knew it would have been easier to ride his horse to the scene this morning, but he was weary of horses after his fall at the Battle of Sharpsburg.

After unbuttoning his coat to relieve himself from the heat, he began to review the notes he took this morning. The empty case disturbed him. He wondered if the orders were taken by the murderer, believing they may be worth something, or if the courier was killed solely for the documents. He was scared to admit the latter, because he knew that meant a more serious matter was afoot. But Thomas, being the professional he was, didn't want to jump to any conclusions. He would first learn the victim's name and see what his orders were last night. This meant he would have to pay the general a visit.

Chapter 2

He felt accomplished as he lit the sweet-smelling tobacco in his pipe. After taking the first long draw, he gazed out of the window onto the street below. Rhett noticed the citizens and soldiers occupying the street didn't seem worried about their city falling to the enemy who lie just off its shores. He hoped that would change soon. He stepped away from the window and over to the wash basin in the middle of the room. Taking the knife from the sheath on his belt, he began to wash it. The dried blood from the Bowie leached into the water, turning it a light red hue. After drying the blade with an old newspaper, he placed it into his nightstand drawer. The two-page order he removed from the courier's case still sat folded on his bed. Having read the document three times, he was confident he knew its contents. He picked it up, crumpled it, and tossed it into the fireplace. Rhett watched in silence as the fire turned the document into a light gray ash.

He put on his clothes after finishing his pipe. A black suit with a dark necktie was his usual attire, but today was different. Feeling a sense of excitement at the information he had gained, he wore a yellow necktie. The brighter color mirrored his sunny mood.

He left his room and descended the stairs into the tailor shop. Mr. Brenton was in the back working, so Rhett didn't bother him. Usually, he would say hello to his landlord before leaving, but not today.

The short walk to the Bank of Charleston gave him time to clear his thoughts and prepare his mind for work. He had been employed there as a loan officer for the past three months as a cover. Well-forged documents provided him with all the credentials he needed to gain the position, as was planned by his superiors. But the world of finance wasn't foreign to Rhett. He had studied business at Yale before being expelled in 1861. His studies must have taken hold, because the bank president seemed more than pleased with his performance. His reputation was so good, in fact, he was able to acquire a part-time position with the provost marshal of the city, Colonel John Marlow. Rhett was paid by the colonel to be his personal bookkeeper. Secretly, the colonel required someone who could keep track of his far-reaching- and sometimes questionable-business dealings. Luckily for Rhett, this relationship was just what he needed. Having access to the colonel's office provided a way to obtain confidential military information. There was a catch, though: he was instructed to keep his position a secret. Marlow told him their work was strictly confidential. And Rhett, being a spy, had no problem keeping secrets.

He walked into the lobby of the bank where he was met by the usual guard. "Good morning, Frederick," Rhett greeted.

"Morning, Mr. LaCroix," Fredrick replied.

Making his way through the well-furnished lobby, Rhett entered his office, which was located a short distance behind the teller windows. He closed the door and placed his briefcase under the desk. He knew he would have a few minutes to himself before the mostly broke city citizens would be asking to speak with him about loans. In truth, Rhett tried his best to be a good employee for the sake of professionalism, but by night, he would perform his real job: Union army spy. That was his real passion, his real career.

He hadn't settled in long before there was a knock at the door. "Come in," he said to the unknown visitor. The door opened to reveal an older man with white hair. He wore a tailored suit, black in color, which was in much better shape than the threadbare rags most of the city's men were forced to wear recently.

"Good morning, Mr. Hiott," Rhett greeted, standing up to shake his boss's hand.

"Just checking on you, Rhett. How many loans have you approved this week?"

"Three so far, sir."

Mr. Hiott raised an eyebrow at the number. "Very good. I must say I've been very pleased with your work."

"Thank you, sir. I just hope I can continue to perform well."

"I'm sure you will," Mr. Hiott replied, taking a short pause to rub his chin. "I would like to invite you to a ball tonight. I think it would be a good time for you to meet some prospective clients."

Rhett smiled and gave a bow. "Thank you for the invitation. I'd be more than honored to attend."

"Our social gatherings may not be as exquisite as the ones you are used to in New Orleans, but I think you may enjoy yourself."

"Thank you, sir."

Mr. Hiott gave a nod before leaving the office.

Rhett was from Baton Rouge, not New Orleans. But his forged resumé listed that he worked in a bank there prior to being forced out by the Union Army's capture of the city. He tried to avoid any talk of New

Orleans since he knew nothing of the place. He knew the mistake of giving incorrect information about his background could raise some suspicions concerning his story.

Needing a smoke, he pulled his pipe out of his briefcase. He packed it with the special Virginia tobacco he had purchased at a small shop in the city market. It was hard to obtain due to the blockade of the harbor. He kicked his feet up on his desk, lit the pipe, and began to puff. He was pleased at how good this assignment was turning out. Having access to Colonel Marlow's office had given him a wealth of information, but it didn't provide everything he needed. This being the case, a knife occasionally had to be pulled—like last night. He didn't mind killing though; he enjoyed it. This being the reason he was expelled from Yale. An unfortunate disagreement with another student ended with him slitting the boy's throat. That was his first kill. Rhett was clever enough to cover his tracks to avoid prosecution, but the college president still believed he was guilty. That was enough to end his studies there. The only thing to do then was join the Union Army. Although from Louisiana, he had no desire to fight for the South. His parents were staunch Unionists before they were killed in a shipwreck while fleeing the new Confederate government. Knowing they wouldn't have left if Louisiana had stayed loyal to the Union, Rhett's greatest desire was to destroy the Confederacy and to end the government that indirectly ended his parent's lives.

Leaning back in his soft cushioned office chair, Rhett smoked for a few more minutes. He then put the pipe down and pulled a sheet of paper from the drawer. He began to scribe a short pass he would give to the sentries at the edge of town this evening:

Allow Mr. LaCroix to exit and re-enter the city tonight. He is under orders from this office to deliver correspondence.

John Marlow, Col.

Rhett had practiced signing the Colonel's name many times. The forgery was exact. Folding it twice, he placed into his coat pocket.

He got up from his chair and walked into the lobby. Moving past the teller windows, he saw a middle-aged man wearing a faded brown suit. The gentleman sat in a chair clutching a bundle of papers under his right arm. Seeing a potential client, Rhett approached him and cordially inquired if he needed any assistance. "Good morning, sir. May I assist you with something?"

The man seemed nervous as he replied, "I need to see someone about a loan. I'm currently in need of capital to keep my business open. The war has placed a heavy strain on my finances."

Rhett smiled before offering the man a handshake. "I'm just the man you need to see. My name is Rhett LaCroix. I'm a loan officer here."

The man gave a forced smile. "Then I'm glad to make your acquaintance, Mr. LaCroix."

Rhett put his hand on the man's shoulder in a gesture of kindness. "Let me assure you that I will do anything I can to help. The Yankees have made all our lives hard. I pray they're defeated soon."

Chapter 3

Thomas arrived at General Ripley's headquarters. The impressive red brick structure was located not far from the provost marshal's office. It was a hub of activity, as most of the administration of the army took place there. Wagons and buggies constantly cluttered the street in front of the building, dropping off and picking up high-ranking officers. Civilian authorities from the city and state were coming and going as well, making the building appear as the center of all power on the peninsula. As for its most prominent tenant, General Ripley, oversaw all military operations within the district. His scope of control included the batteries and forts surrounding the harbor, as well as the city itself. The courier murdered last night had worked for him.

"Can I help you, Captain?" a young lieutenant asked Thomas as he entered the building.

"I need to speak with the general about the death of one of his couriers. Is he here presently?"

"He is, sir. May I ask your name?"

"Captain Thomas Altman. I'm with the provost marshal."

"Thank you, sir," the lieutenant replied, before scurrying down the hallway.

Thomas waited no less than thirty seconds before the lieutenant reappeared. "He will see you now, sir. Please come this way."

The lieutenant motioned Thomas into a hallway and followed close behind him. "Last door on the left, sir."

Thomas heard him but didn't respond. He walked into the last office where he found General Ripley sitting behind his desk. The commander was dressed in a white cotton shirt buttoned to the top. He held a large cigar with his right hand. The left was busy twirling one side of his long mustache, and his eyes were focused on several documents on his desk.

"Excuse me, sir," Thomas said, standing at attention.

The general looked up. He blew out a cloud of thick smoke before acknowledging Thomas. "What can I do for you, Captain?"

Thomas felt nervous. He had never addressed a general. "I've come to speak with you about the death of one of your couriers, sir."

The general leaned back in his chair, still pulling on his whiskers. He put the cigar on the lip of the ashtray. "Have a seat."

Thomas sat in the chair in front of the general. It was extremely comfortable and far nicer than the rickety seat he was forced to use as a desk chair.

"You work for Marlow?" Ripley asked.

"Yes sir, I do."

"You aren't a West Pointer?"

"No, sir. I graduated from The Citadel shortly after the capture of Fort Sumter."

Ripley nodded. "Any battlefield experience?"

Thomas didn't see where this was going but answered the general's question without hesitation. "I was at the Battle of Sharpsburg, sir. A fall from my horse during a charge ended my career in the field."

Thomas's knee was nearly mangled from the fall. He was sent home to Charleston to recuperate. After he was healed enough to return to duty, his superiors assigned him to work for the provost marshal. In truth, he believed the injury to be somewhat of a blessing. He was glad he wasn't sent back to General Lee's army in Virginia. He loved his new job.

"Well then, it's good to meet you," the general complimented. "I'm forced to deal with many who've never seen combat. The army has more than its fair share of cowards, Captain."

"Thank you, sir."

The general picked up his cigar from the ashtray and took a long pull before holding it loosely in his hand. "Now about the death of my courier, Private James Fowler."

Now Thomas knew the name of the victim. He made a quick mental note to write it down when he left the office. "Yes, sir. Can you tell me what his orders were last night?"

Ripley shook his head in a disappointed manner. "He was carrying correspondence addressed to the commander at Fort Wagner. The documents advised him of some cannons and troops I'm sending to reinforce the place."

"Would this document be valuable to the enemy, sir?"

The general began to look uneasy now. He slowly leaned forward in his chair and gazed at Thomas. "They would be more than valuable, Captain. We don't want the Yankees knowing that we are weakening one fort to reinforce another. Those orders were very detailed as to our plan for defending Morris Island." After pausing a moment to draw on his cigar, he continued, "If Private

Fowler was killed for those orders, that is most distressing."

"I'm sure I speak for Colonel Marlow when I say we will do all we can, sir," Thomas insured.

The general gave a half smile. "Very good, Captain. Please keep me updated on any findings."

Thomas stood up to leave. "I will, sir. Have a good day."

Almost to the door, the general stopped him. "Captain."

Thomas turned around. "Yes, sir?"

"The president of the Bank of Charleston is giving a ball tonight to honor of our defense of the city. I would like you to show up if you can. Perhaps you may speak of your combat experiences in Virginia."

"Thank you, sir. I will do my best to attend."

Thomas exited the smoky office into the hallway. At the front door, he saw Colonel Marlow climbing down from his horse. Thomas noticed his superior didn't look happy to see him.

"What are you doing here, Altman?" the colonel asked gruffly, while tying his horse to the hitching post.

"Speaking to the general about the murder of the courier, sir."

The colonel took off his hat and wiped his forehead with his sleeve. His silver hair was soaked with sweat. "I wish you would have told me you were coming here. I wanted to know what information the general was able to provide."

Thomas knew the colonel really didn't care about the murder. He only wanted to be a part of the investigation because it dealt with the general's man.

"I'm sorry, sir," Thomas apologized. "I only thought it best to gather information as quickly as possible. You said this was a high priority."

The colonel shook his head and put his hat back on. "I know I said that, but I want to be kept informed on what you learn. Do you understand me?"

"Yes, sir."

The colonel then moved quickly into the headquarters building. He didn't wait for Thomas to salute him.

As he made his way back to the provost marshal's headquarters, Thomas began to feel guilty. He had lied to General Ripley. The truth was this: he wasn't wounded charging his horse toward the enemy at the Battle of Sharpsburg; he was riding away. Retreating without orders actually—running away. The horse he was riding threw a shoe during his escape from the battlefield, sending him crashing into a tree. He had contributed nothing to the army on the one and only day he had experienced real fighting. Since then, Thomas felt like a coward, scared to die for the cause. The limp he was forced to walk with every day provided a constant reminder of his disgraceful behavior. But he pledged to himself to never show cowardice again.

Thomas saw Lieutenant Chase making his way hastily toward him about a block from the provost building.

"I've been looking all over for you, sir!" Chase exclaimed.

"What is it, Lieutenant?"

Chase tried to calm himself before answering. He took a deep breath. "There's a witness to the courier's murder, sir. She's in your office now."

Thomas felt his heart beat faster. He didn't think there would be a witness. "Let's go," he ordered, already moving.

The two men quickly made it there. Thomas was anxious to learn about this new information and hoped it could be the lead he needed to identify the suspect. But when he and Chase arrived, his office was empty.

Thomas turned to the Lieutenant. "Where is she?"

Chase looked bewildered. "I don't know, sir. She was right here. I told her I was going to get you right away."

"What about a name?" Thomas asked, hoping at least for that.

"Her name was Louise, sir. She said she was a house slave on East Bay Street. Her master's last name was Jones."

Thomas was more than disappointed she wasn't there, but at least he could find her. After scribing a short note to the colonel telling him of the new development, he handed it to Chase. "Go upstairs and put this on the colonel's desk. He wants to know everything we find out about this murder."

"Yes, sir."

Chase took the note from Thomas and disappeared into the hallway.

Thomas took a seat at his desk. He wrote down the same information he gave to the colonel on a small slip of paper and put it in his coat pocket. He knew the excitement of a lead wouldn't allow him to stay in the office today. He was going to find this woman, now. But as he was readying to leave, a young blonde-haired private in a butternut-colored uniform appeared in his doorway. The soldier snapped to attention and saluted him.

Thomas returned the salute. "Can I help you, Private?"

"I have a message from General Ripley, sir."

The private handed Thomas a calling card with the general's name on the front. Turning it over, there was an address and a time:

129 King Street – Seven o'clock

"Thank you, Private," Thomas said, gesturing the soldier away.

Lieutenant Chase returned to the office just as the private made his way out. "Delivered the note, sir. He can't miss it where it sits on his desk. Are we going to look for the witness now?"

Thomas wanted to. In fact, he wanted to very much. But he knew an invitation from a general was not really an invitation; it was an order. Knowing it best not to insult one of the most powerful men in the city, he would have to put finding the witness on hold. After all, she would be there when the ball was over anyway.

Chapter 4

Rhett was trying to hurry. Leaving the bank, he headed for Colonel Marlow's office. He had to make several entries into the colonel's books before he could get ready for this evening's ball. He was under strict instructions not to enter the provost marshal building during normal hours. Since his part-time employment dealt with illegal monetary gains, the colonel didn't want any of the normal army personnel to see him in the building.

After weaving his way through Charleston's busy afternoon streets, he entered the building through the rear door. Climbing the staircase to the second floor, he put his ear to the door leading into the hallway to hear if anyone remained inside. The colonel was specific: *do not be seen.* Hearing no one, he opened the stairwell door and made his way out. Rhett proceeded to the colonel's office, which bore the man's name in small white letters on the door: *J. Marlow*. He entered and locked the door behind him. Before Rhett sat down, he removed his coat and loosened his necktie. He pulled out a pile of documents from the bottom drawer and put them on the desk. The documents were receipts and promissory notes that he had to account for in the ledger. It was then something caught his eye, something that was unusual. A small folded note sat on the far corner of the desk. It appeared to have been placed there in a manner for the colonel to read it immediately. Like any other document in the office, Rhett would examine it to see if it had any military importance. Opening it, he read:

Sir,

Possible witness named Louise in the courier murder. She's a house servant in the Jones residence on East Bay Street. Will investigate further in the morning.

Altman

Rhett refolded the paper and put it back down. His heart began to race, his breathing deeper than usual. He quickly thought about what would happen should he be identified—public death by hanging. His downfall would be used by the rebels as propaganda. It would be a display of what would happen to anyone spying for the Union. Composing himself, he stood up and put his jacket back on. After checking his appearance in the colonel's mirror, he made a hasty exit from the office. He left the building as he entered, quiet and cautious, now making for his room located on the upper end of King Street. He pulled his silver pocket watch from his vest and checked the time—six o'clock. He had planned on a quiet evening in a tavern after the ball, but those plans had changed. The slave on East Bay Street had to be handled. He couldn't allow her to be questioned in the morning. He moved past the other citizens without noticing them. Several of the men tipped their hats, but he didn't return the gesture. Focusing on what he had to do tonight made him oblivious to the world around him. He seemed to float across the cobblestone streets that usually had to be traversed with caution.

Arriving at his lodgings, he entered the tailor shop. Mr. Brenton was behind the counter sewing a pair of trousers. "Good evening, Mr. Brenton," Rhett greeted, before walking through the shop and up the stairs. Although he knew it was rude, he didn't wait for his landlord to respond.

In his room, he quickly changed into his best suit; it was light brown with a black tie. Rhett pulled open the nightstand drawer and took out his sheathed Bowie knife. He tucked it into the rear of his trousers, as was its normal carrying position. He grabbed the forged pass he wrote for himself earlier and slipped it into his pocket before leaving. He looked again at his watch—twenty minutes.

Back down the stairs and into the shop, he saw Mr. Brenton standing in the doorway. It looked as if he was purposely blocking Rhett's passage.

"Why such a hurry, Rhett?" the tailor asked, wiping his silver rimmed spectacles with a cloth.

"I must make a social engagement, Mr. Brenton. I apologize if I was rude earlier."

Mr. Brenton put his spectacles back on and adjusted them on the bridge of his nose. "You weren't rude. I was just wanting to know if you needed any food brought up to your room this evening."

Rhett truly appreciated the gesture, but he knew he wouldn't need it. "Unfortunately, I will be out very late this evening, sir. I don't expect to be back until the early hours of the morning." And he wasn't lying. Rhett had much to do before the sun came up.

Chapter 5

Thomas arrived in front of the large white mansion. Its massive size and beauty amazed him. It was, without question, one of the nicest homes in the city. Having passed by it many times when he was younger, he had always wondered who was so fortunate to possess such a home. He was met by a servant dressed in a black suit on the porch.

"May I help you, sir?" the servant politely asked, giving Thomas a bow.

"I'm here on the invitation of General Ripley," Thomas replied.

"Very good, sir. Please come this way."

The servant opened the door and motioned Thomas to step inside. Entering a large foyer, he removed his hat and gave it to the servant.

"Follow the hall down, Captain. You will find the rest of the guests in the ballroom," the servant advised.

He soon found himself in the doorway of a large, lavish assembly room. He surveyed the space and quickly realized he was severely underdressed. His faded gray uniform was nothing in comparison to the expensive dress suits the civilian men were wearing.

"I'm glad you're here, Captain!" a voice called from his left.

Thomas turned to see General Ripley with a lit cigar in one hand and a glass of whiskey in the other. He came to attention and gave a quick salute. "Thank you for inviting me, sir. I'm honored to have called on your invitation."

The general gave a quick wink before responding, "Thank you, son. Now, let me introduce you to our benefactor, Mr. Hiott."

The general led Thomas across the ballroom. That's when he caught a glimpse of a young woman standing in the corner. He was struck by her beauty. She was in her early twenties, same as he, and wore a green dress with a white sash. Her auburn-colored hair flowed down past her shoulders in ringlets. As she turned to meet his gaze, Thomas averted his eyes for fear she would catch him staring. The two men passed the pianist whose fingers were busy working the keys. Thomas thought he heard the man playing one of Chopin's nocturnes, which was a type of music seldom heard now in Charleston. Most of the talented musicians had already left the city for more hospitable, and far less dangerous, locales.

Thomas and Ripley stopped in front of a small man who appeared to be in his early sixties. The gentleman was surrounded by guests who seemed attentive to his every word. "This is Mr. Calvin Hiott, Captain," Ripley said, grabbing the man's attention away from the other guests.

"Pleased to meet you, sir," Thomas said as the two shook hands.

"It's a pleasure, Captain. The general tells me you work for John Marlow."

"I do, sir."

A slight smirk appeared on Mr. Hiott's face. Thomas could tell this was not an expression of admiration. Colonel Marlow was rumored to be disliked by some of the upper-class citizens, but for what reasons, he was unaware.

"Well then," Mr. Hiott began, "I must admit I've never been fond of the man, but I'm told he performs his military duties well." He looked over to General Ripley. "And that's what we need in this city. Men who perform their duties well. Right, General?"

"Absolutely, sir," General Ripley replied with a gentle nod.

Mr. Hiott turned back to Thomas. "I want to show the officers here that we appreciate their hard work keeping the Yankees at bay. That's why I threw this ball tonight. You men deserve a good time away from the front lines."

"Thank you, sir. Your generosity is appreciated," Thomas replied.

Mr. Hiott and the general stepped away to speak to some other guests, leaving Thomas alone in the middle of the ballroom floor. Retreating to a less conspicuous empty table in the corner, a servant approached him and asked if he desired a drink. Thomas requested a glass of whiskey, which the servant fetched in less than a minute. He took a few swigs of the spirit and looked around the room. The lowest-ranking man present, he felt strangely out of place. He considered slipping out once he had the first chance, but he didn't want to offend General Ripley. It was an affront he knew he couldn't risk. It was then he noticed a civilian enter the ballroom. The man was well dressed, wearing a well-tailored brown suit. Although he looked like the rest of the guests, Thomas felt there was something different about him. He didn't seem relaxed. When he moved, it was in a nervous fashion, anxious even? The man was tall with dark black hair, and his mustache was long and pointed at the ends. Thomas kept his eye on him as the man made his way to Mr. Hiott. The two shook hands before beginning to speak, alluding that they clearly knew each other. This being this case, he gave no further thought to the matter.

Scanning the room again, he saw her. It was the woman in the green dress. To his surprise, she was looking at him. Feeling it was a sign she shared his desire to converse with one another, he put down his glass and began to make his way across the shiny floor. He tried not limp as he walked. The injury had garnered unwanted sympathy from people in the past and he cared nothing for it.

She smiled at Thomas when he was a few feet away.

"Good evening, ma'am. Captain Thomas Altman," he said, giving her a small bow.

The woman smiled and bowed slightly in return. "I'm Ellen Hiott. It's a pleasure to meet you."

"Are you related to the gentlemen giving this affair? Hiott? As in Mr. Calvin Hiott?"

"Yes, Captain. He's my father."

Thomas was slightly intimidated by her status. She would surely be considered a belle of Charleston society. He worried a woman like that may not want to speak with a low-ranking officer, but he decided to see where the conversation led anyway. "Then I assume this marvelous residence is home as well?"

"It is in indeed."

Thomas looked up at the ceiling and around the room. "You are quite fortunate then. I must admit that I've always admired this house."

Ellen glanced over at her father who was deep in conversation with two army men. "It seems my father is playing host now. I can show you around if you'd like."

Thomas was eager to talk with her further. He wasn't going to pass up the chance to do so. "I would like that very much."

Ellen put her left hand inside Thomas's bent arm. "This way, Captain."

She led him out of the ballroom and into the dining room. His attention was drawn to an expensive chandelier hanging from the ceiling just above a large mahogany dining table. The table was large enough for twelve guests but had settings for only two.

"Only my father and I dine here, usually. My mother is currently away," Ellen said.

"Where has she gone?" Thomas asked.

Ellen dropped her head. "Just away for a while. It's a bit of long story."

Thomas could sense she was uncomfortable speaking of her mother. He tried to change the subject quickly. "Perhaps we should get some fresh air?"

"Yes, Captain," she answered. "Fresh air would be nice."

She led him through the house to the back door. The two descended a short flight of stairs into a garden that was illuminated by several dozen lanterns.

"I love walking through here at night," Ellen said. "It's so peaceful when the cannons of Fort Sumter are silent."

That's when Thomas heard the sound—cannon fire. It was ironic that Ellen just spoke of this. They stopped and looked at each other, both aware of what this meant. The ball would be ending now.

"Thank you for showing me around, Miss Hiott. Not to sound too forward, but I would like to call on you again if I may."

Ellen released his arm and turned to him. Her face was just barely visible through the darkness. "You may call on me, Captain. In fact, I hope you do so."

Thomas bowed to her before heading back inside. He was moving quickly now, the guns of the fort alerting all military men that an attack was occurring. In the foyer, the nervous civilian he saw talking to Mr. Hiott bumped into him. Thomas stood there briefly waiting on an apology, but the man ran out the door without acknowledging him. He thought it was rude, but he knew the cannon fire had unnerved everyone. He let the matter go. Retrieving his hat from the servant's stand, he ventured out into the darkness to find soldiers running in the direction of the harbor. He started toward his battle station. Although an administrative officer, he was assigned to the Fraser's Wharf Battery should an attack on the city occur.

After a trip on foot of no less than twenty minutes, he arrived there in a moderate amount of pain. His desire for a fight had pushed him faster than his knee could handle. He stopped for a moment at the battery entrance to take a short rest before finding the commander. That's when he heard the cannon fire slowing, which he knew to be a good sign.

"Captain Altman!" a voice called out.

Thomas looked toward the battery entrance to see someone running his way. He called him again, "Captain!"

Once the man got closer, Thomas could see it was Lieutenant Chase. "Chase, what's happening?"

The lieutenant stopped briefly to salute. "Some ironclads tried to run the harbor, but they couldn't get past Sumter."

Thomas was disappointed he couldn't help man the guns. There had been no chance for redemption after his cowardly retreat at Sharpsburg. He had wanted to prove to himself that he could truly face the enemy. "What's the battery commander saying?" he asked.

"He's relieving us, sir. We've been ordered to stand down."

Realizing the night didn't have to be completely unproductive, Thomas remembered he still needed to question the witness who was at his office earlier. The home of her master was less than three blocks away.

"Accompany me to see the woman who came by today," he said to Chase. "I'd like to learn what she knows."

"Yes, sir. Would you like me to grab some horses?"

Although Thomas's knee needed a rest, he hated riding. "Let's walk it, Lieutenant. There shouldn't be any need for horses tonight."

Chapter 6

Rhett was glad his Navy tried to run the ring of forts surrounding Charleston Harbor. The fire from the gunboats was the distraction he needed to keep him from looking suspicious. The battle had caused the usual panic. People were running to and from different locations in a hurried and excited manner. This being the case, his hustled walk to East Bay Street didn't seem as suspicious as it normally would.

By the time the guns fell silent, he had made it to the home of Randall Jones, a prominent attorney in the city. Mr. Hiott had introduced him to Mr. Jones at the ball, and through a little conversation, Rhett learned he had a servant named Louise. He couldn't believe his luck. Concerned about having to go house to house to learn of the servant's location, he was more than happy it worked out this way. He crossed to the other side of the street where he found a dark alley to stand in. Not knowing what the woman looked like, he wanted to be sure he chose the right target. But Rhett didn't know what he would do even if he found her. He couldn't kick the door in and kill her. That would be too dangerous, too messy. Needing some time to think, he took out his pipe and packed it. After lighting the tobacco and taking a few puffs, Rhett saw a figure walk up to the residence. He could tell it was a woman by the way she moved, but he couldn't tell anything else. The darkness obscured any of her features. The figure didn't go up the steps. She went through a wooden gate on the south side of the house. Rhett assumed the gate led to the back yard. Knowing that most homes had slave quarters in the rear, he believed he may have found his prey. He knocked the half-spent tobacco out of his pipe and placed it in his jacket pocket. He crossed the street and came to the gate through which the figure entered. It was a white picket fence with a latch that creaked loudly as he operated it. The sound slowed him, but it didn't stop him. He surveyed the yard. A small cabin with a planked roof sat in the back corner of the property, several yards from the main house. A candle was burning brightly through one of the front windows. He moved cautiously through the darkness over to the shack. Putting his ear to wall, he heard:

"I went by there, mama, but the man who I needed to see was gone."

"Go on back tomorrow, child. I'll tell Mister Jones you goin' for some flour."

He pulled his ear away. He had heard enough. The younger woman was to be his victim. Although normal men would have reservations about killing an innocent woman, Rhett had none. He had to protect his cover at all costs. Reaching down between his feet, he picked up a small rock. He tossed it at the window on the cabin, hoping the younger of the two women would step outside to investigate the sound. The front door creaked open a moment later. He reached behind his back and pulled the Bowie knife from its sheath. Gripping it hard so as not to lose it after the first stab, he moved slowly around the corner to find a young Negro woman standing outside. It happened fast. One thrust of the knife to the woman's stomach dropped her to the ground. But he didn't anticipate his victim screaming before he made the assault. It was loud. The older woman in the cabin came out responding to the scream. He was just pulling the knife from the girl's body when the other woman attacked him. A combination of punches and kicks caught him off guard, but not so much as to incapacitate him. With one slash of his knife, the woman screamed and ran to the main house. He didn't know how badly he had injured her, or if he had cut her at all, but it was enough to send her fleeing for help. He put his knife back into its sheath and took one more look at his victim—no movement. Satisfied she was dead, he made his way back to the gate. Rhett was running this time though, entirely in contrast to his slow entrance a few minutes earlier. He reached for the latch. He was mad at himself for closing it, knowing he should have left it open to hasten his departure.

Chapter 7

Thomas made better time getting to the Jones residence than he expected. His main concern was that it was too late to call on the witness. But the matter couldn't wait. The capture of this villain was far too important.

"Which house is it, sir?" Chase asked.

"I'm not sure," Thomas answered, "but we have to find it."

They located the house after a few minutes of going door to door. It was a two-story brick home with a large front porch. The name *R. Jones* was painted on a wooden plank by the door. They ascended the steps and Thomas knocked twice. It was almost a minute before someone answered. It was Mr. Jones. Thomas was familiar with the well-known lawyer.

"Good evening, sir. I'm Captain Altman with the provost marshal's office," Thomas greeted. "What's the meaning of this, Captain?" Mr. Jones asked.

Thomas could tell Mr. Jones didn't want them there. The look on the lawyer's face was one of irritation. But the matter had to be pressed. "I'm investigating the murder of a soldier. One of your servants came by our office today to give us some information about the crime. Unfortunately, I wasn't at my office when she arrived. I was hoping I may speak to her now."

"That's interesting," Mr. Jones replied, raising his eyebrows curiously. "I never gave her permission to go to *your*, or any other, government office. Furthermore, she hasn't told me anything about a murder."

Thomas cringed. He realized he had just put this witness into an awkward position. Disobedience to a slave's master was handled in different ways, but he sensed Mr. Jones was the type to take a heavy-handed approach to discipline. "I wasn't looking to cause any problems in your household, sir, but I can assure you this matter is of the utmost importance," he explained. "It is imperative I speak with her now."

"Very well, Captain," Mr. Jones answered, mildly relenting. "But I ask that you keep this conversation short. I have to get up early in the morning to attend court."

The two men were shown inside. After removing their hats, Thomas looked around, amazed at the size of the residence. It was small in comparison to Mr. Hiott's home, but still quite impressive.

"I've already let the servants retire to their quarters. Give me a moment to fetch them from the back." Mr. Jones said, before pointing to a sitting room to the left. "You may have a seat while you are waiting."

"Thank you, sir," both men replied.

They took seats in two identical high-backed chairs. Thomas's eye was quickly drawn to a rug on the floor. He admired its intricate pattern, thinking it must have been one of the expensive Persian kinds he had only heard about. He thought of how only a few of the city's residents were able to possess such rare and exotic things. But his thoughts abruptly stopped when he heard a female scream. He and Chase leaped from the chairs and ran toward the sound. It came from outside near the back of the house.

"Go out the front door, I'll head to the back," Thomas ordered Chase.

The young lieutenant did as he was told, racing to the front door and making his way down the steps.

Thomas ran through the house frantically searching for the way to the back. Making it through the dining room, he at last came to an open door. He heard another scream, this one just as loud as the first. Thomas made his way outside and into the backyard to find Mr. Jones huddled over something on the ground. Behind him was a Negro woman crying loudly. Before Thomas could make it there, he heard a loud creaking noise just to his left. He looked over to see a gate opening, followed by a dark figure moving through.

"Chase!" Thomas yelled as loud as he could.

Turning to pursue the suspect, Thomas yelled again, "Chase!" He hoped his aide was still in front, as the person was making a hasty retreat toward the street. Through the gate he ran. He pulled his revolver from his holster knowing the assailant may be armed. But as he did so, Thomas lost sight of the shadowy figure.

"Captain!" Chase yelled.

"Over here!" Thomas called back. There was no answer. He made it to the street where he slowed for a moment to look for Chase. It was then he heard a gunshot—it was close. Running to the sound, he saw something on the ground in the entrance to an alley. To his horror, it was Chase. The lieutenant was not moving, and his revolver was laying on the ground near his hand. Thomas checked to see if he was still breathing—he was. Examining him further, Thomas discovered a wound on his left arm. It was bleeding heavily. He took off his belt and wrapped it tightly around the arm, as he would a tourniquet. He then called out for anyone who was listening, "Help!" He called again, louder this time, "Please help!"

The gunshot must have alarmed some of the residents, because several people were there within seconds. Thomas continued to hold the belt tight until a police constable and two soldiers arrived. Seeing what was happening, the constable told him he would get a doctor there immediately.

A few tense minutes later, a doctor arrived, dressed in his nightshirt, carrying a medical bag. Thomas backed away allowing the man to tend to Chase. He then approached the police constable who was standing nearby. "I need you to get word to Inspector James to meet me here."

The constable eyed Thomas curiously. "The victim is a soldier, sir. What's the reason to bring the inspector?"

"A good reason!" Thomas spat. "There's been a murder at the residence of Randall Jones. The name alone should get him here quickly."

The constable's expression quickly changed to one of surprise. "I understand, sir," he replied, before running off.

Thomas turned back to the doctor now. "Is he alright, sir?"

The doctor shook his head. "We need to get him to a surgeon. It's all I can do to try and control the bleeding."

"I'll get my buggy!" a voice called out from the crowd.

"Please, hurry!" Thomas called back.

As he waited for the conveyance to arrive, Thomas realized he was up against something more than just a murderer. A man who would go to such lengths as to find and kill a witness was not the type of man he was used to investigating. There was something different about this, he was sure of it.

Chapter 8

Rhett was running as fast as his feet would carry him. Sweating profusely, breathing heavily - his desire to elude capture was the only thing keeping him going.

Arriving at the tailor's shop, he took the key from his pocket and unlocked the front door. He made his way past the clothing racks and up the staircase to his room. His shaky hand unlocked the door and he entered inside. Before doing anything else, he reached for the knife and unsheathed it. Fresh blood covered the blade from the tip to the base. The sight of the stained weapon made him realize just what he had done. Killing the witness to prohibit her from identifying him was a necessity, but the killing of the soldier was not. This would only increase the authorities' efforts to find him.

He washed his blood-soaked hands in the wash basin before cleaning his knife. Taking a seat, he continued to reflect on what happened—how it didn't go as planned. He hoped the two soldiers being there was a mere coincidence. The note left on the colonel's desk said the slave would be spoken to in the morning, not tonight. *Did they know my intentions?* he wondered. His thoughts changed again. He remembered knocking the officer's hand away before the trigger was pulled. One second slower and he would have been killed. He knew he was lucky this time.

Rhett reached for his suit jacket hanging on the back of the chair. He had always been able to think clearer during a session with his pipe. He pulled out a small paper pouch of tobacco from the left pocket and put it on the desk. He then slipped his hand into the other pocket to retrieve his pipe, but it wasn't there. The dual emotions of anger and fear rushed over him like a wave. He picked up the inkwell from the desk and threw it across the room. The bottle shattered against the wall, causing the black sticky substance to drip onto the floor. This was a disaster, and he knew it. Placing his head into his hands, he sat quietly until the moment passed. His anger and fear now turned to disappointment. He was disappointed at himself for performing sloppy work. Somehow the pipe had been dropped while he was fighting the soldier in the alley. *Could it be traced to me?* he thought. The pipe had a small engraving of a fleur-de-lis on the bottom of the bowl. Although not a specific mark, such as a person's initials, he knew it could be used to identify the pipe as different from any other. He wondered what he should do now. To escape to the Union lines would save his life. He could explain that his cover was becoming comprised and it was necessary to leave the city. This would have been acceptable to his superiors, but he wasn't going to do that. Failure was not an option.

He put his jacket back on. After tucking the sheathed knife back in his trousers, he made his way down the stairs and into the street. He had to get back to see if he could retrieve the pipe. Knowing the darkness would make it hard to see anything lying on the ground, he held out hope that it was still there. The authorities now surrounding the area may have missed it—or so he hoped.

Once there, he grew even more concerned. Several constables, along with a few soldiers, were shining lanterns everywhere, looking near the alley. *Maybe they won't find it,* he continued to tell himself. He tried to blend in with the crowd of citizens as he observed, realizing the authorities would never believe the assailant was still there. He believed this approach to be so overt, it was covert. Still disappointed by these events, there seemed to be a bit of good news. The soldier he stabbed was no longer present. He hoped he cut him deep enough to kill him. Because if the man lived, he knew he would be busy yet again. There would be one more witness to eliminate.

After a few minutes, he slowly pushed his way to the front of the crowd for a better view. That's when he saw the one thing he didn't want to see. An army officer, along with a man whom he assumed to be a member of the police force, were crouching near the entrance to the alley. The man in civilian clothes ordered a constable to bring two lanterns over. When the constable lit the area, he saw the army officer lift something off the ground. It was his pipe.

"I can't believe someone killed Mr. Jones's servant," a voice said.

Rhett was so focused on the two men finding his pipe, he didn't notice the people around him. He turned to his right to find an elderly woman dressed entirely in black. He knew he had to respond to what she said, so as not to seem suspicious. "It's a shame, ma'am. The city becomes more dangerous as the war goes on."

The woman shook her head. "I'm glad to see that soldier wasn't dead when they carried him off. Two deaths in one night on the same street—that's just too much."

Again, Rhett felt his heart drop into his stomach.

"I just arrived here, ma'am. You said the soldier was alive?" he asked again. He wanted to be sure he heard her correctly.

"That's what I was told. My husband and I came as quickly as possible after hearing the gunshot. The soldier was lucky my husband is a doctor. He may have already been dead if that wasn't the case," the woman said, taking a short pause. "Do you live close, sir? I thought I knew all my neighbors, but I don't know you."

"Have a good evening, ma'am," Rhett said, tipping his top hat as he walked away.

Back at his room, he changed from his suit into something more fitted for riding. After donning his brown coat, slouch hat, and riding boots, he took the forged pass out of the nightstand drawer and put it in his pocket. He still had to deliver his message to his contact north of the city tonight. He hoped the information he acquired from the dead courier's dispatch case would be valuable to his superiors.

He left the tailor shop and walked two blocks to the civilian stables. It took him several minutes of negotiating a price with the owner, but he eventually rented a black mare with a good set of shoes for the evening. Luckily, the stable owner threw in a lantern for him to use as well. Rhett had not thought about bringing the proper supplies for his journey. The incident tonight on East Bay Street had more than rattled his thinking and distracted him from any preparation.

He rode to the military checkpoint north of the city. He knew the sentries standing guard would let him out without questioning him, but they would be more suspicious when letting him back in. But he wasn't as concerned with the sentries as much as he was with what transpired earlier. He hoped when he made it back, there wouldn't be a gang of police waiting for him at his room.

He met a sergeant holding a lantern at the sentry post. The soldier stood in front of a wooden barricade blocking the road, with his musket resting lazily on his shoulder. "Good evening, Sergeant," he greeted, before giving the pass to the sentry. "I have a pass from Colonel Marlow allowing me out."

The sergeant took the paper and looked at it. Rhett held his breath, hoping the man didn't have any questions. The night had already contained enough difficulties.

The sergeant examined the pass and returned it. "Be careful out there, sir. There's a heap of dangerous folks on the north end of the peninsula," he warned.

"Thank you for the advice," Rhett replied, putting the pass back into his pocket. "I would also like to thank you for keeping the Yankees out of our city."

The sergeant nodded before spitting some tobacco juice onto the ground. "None will get through here on my watch. I'll guarantee that."

Rhett laughed inwardly at the irony of the situation.

Riding out, he began to think about what the sergeant said: the warning about traveling north of town. He had been told by more than one person that the north end of the peninsula contained a myriad of undesirable people. Highwaymen, deserters, and runaway slaves called this part of Charleston home. Rhett decided he would keep his knife close and his horse moving.

After passing through two shanty towns without any issues, he was there. A small, dark cabin on the edge of the river. He hitched the horse to the tree just in front and approached the door. He knew he had to be careful. If his handler had been captured and questioned, there may be Confederate agents waiting on the other side. He knocked twice. The door opened to reveal a man holding a candle, large in stature, wearing a faded green jacket and black riding boots. A large scar ran from his hairline to his cheek, which added to his rugged appearance. The man's name was Joshua Hawkins. He was Rhett's handler and primary contact.

"Were you followed?" Hawkins asked.

Rhett was irritated by the question. He had been a spy long enough to know how to spot someone tailing him. "Of course not! Were you?"

Hawkins smirked but didn't answer. "Come in and have a seat."

Rhett removed his hat and stepped inside. He was more than happy to seek refuge from the insects he had endured on the journey. The numerous mosquito bites he received on his neck and arms had made him quite uncomfortable.

The two men sat down at a table in the center of the room. There was no other furniture, no signs of anyone living there. Hawkins picked up a pewter cup from the table and took a sip before speaking. "The general wants to know about your progress. I'm sure you know the navy has been less than successful at running the forts surrounding the harbor."

Rhett ignored Hawkins's request for information. He pointed at Hawkins's cup. "Do you have any of that for me?"

"No," Hawkins replied casually, before turning it up to finish its contents.

Rhett wasn't thirsty. He asked about the drink only to frustrate Hawkins. In truth, he didn't like the man.

"Don't be obtuse, LaCroix," Hawkins said gruffly. "We have no time for that."

Rhett shrugged. "Very well. I've made a discovery concerning the strength of the forts you've spoken about. The rebel commander has decreased the number of troops in Fort Sumter to reinforce Fort Wagner. I've also learned they've placed two more cannons inside Wagner to help cover its land approaches. They must know we're going to attack there."

Hawkins put his hand to his chin in thought. "That's not good. The plan is to attack Wagner on the eighteenth. We were unaware they had strengthened the defenses."

"I have no other information past that," Rhett continued, "but I'll be able to find out more if given some time."

"We don't have much time," Hawkins retorted. "Your primary objective has changed."

Rhett fidgeted in his seat. This didn't sound good. "Changed how?" he asked.

"You will infiltrate Wagner the night of the attack. Once inside, you will assist our forces in capturing the fort."

Rhett couldn't believe he was being asked to do this. He found the assignment to be impossible, if not suicidal. "What you're asking me to do can't be done," he replied. "I'm believed to be a civilian, not a soldier. I wouldn't be allowed access."

Hawkins shook his head. "There are other men like you, LaCroix. Men who are standing by to take your place if you don't do as you're ordered."

"No man can do what you've asked," Rhett replied, growing angry at the innuendo. "I would need a completely different cover to even attempt that."

Hawkins stared at Rhett with a shifty glare. "I didn't want to have to tell you this, but if you refuse the assignment, you will come with me immediately. Once back with the army, you will be given another, perhaps easier, assignment."

"What type of assignment?" Rhett inquired.

"Field command, I guess," Hawkins answered, shrugging. "We're losing infantry officers faster than we can replace them. Seems as though the rebs like to target the officers instead of the enlisted men."

Rhett was trapped, and he knew it. If he said no, his superiors would make him pay by giving him the worst, if not the most dangerous, command. There was no other choice. "Tell me the details," he said.

Hawkins smiled. "I somehow knew you would say yes; you've made a wise decision."

After an hour of Hawkins explaining the attack plan on Wagner, Rhett felt he understood what needed to be done.

"Any other questions?" Hawkins asked him.

"None," Rhett answered, as he put on his hat and gloves.

Hawkins reached under the table and produced a whiskey bottle. He poured himself a drink as he watched Rhett stand. "Just so you know, I've been keeping an eye on you."

Rhett was confused. He was told that no other spies were allowed in the city. "You aren't supposed to be near me. I was told…"

Hawkins stopped him, "I know what you were told, but there's been some concern that you are too green for this assignment. I was ordered to shadow you to make sure you were on task."

Rhett was offended but tried not to show it. "There'll be no need for shadowing. Everything has gone to plan so far."

"Has it?" Hawkins asked with a small grin.

"What are you implying?" Rhett asked. It was evident Hawkins knew something.

"That was a poor performance on East Bay Street," Hawkins criticized. "You didn't handle that as well as you should have."

He couldn't believe what he was hearing. Hawkins must have followed him to the Jones residence tonight. He was embarrassed now; but also a little irritated that he was being followed. "There were complications, but you've no need to check up on me," he explained. "If you believe I'm incapable of performing my duties, pull me out now."

Hawkins stood up and motioned with his hands for Rhett to settle down. "Easy, LaCroix. If we didn't believe you had the ability to carry out this mission, you would already be gone."

"Then there's no need to follow me any longer. You would agree?"

"I'm just following orders."

Rhett walked to the door and opened it. "Then I bid you adieux, *monsieur*," Rhett said, allowing his native tongue to take over.

Hawkins didn't reply. He stood with his arms folded until Rhett left the cabin.

Chapter 9

Thomas woke up the next morning at the barracks. He had spent most of last night beside Lieutenant Chase's bed. His aide was still unconscious, but there was a bit of good news. The attending physician advised that Chase would fully recover from the laceration without any lasting disability. Thomas was thankful, at least for that. He was also hopeful that Chase saw the assailant's face. To identify the suspect was now his key objective. He believed he was dealing with someone who was more than just a violent citizen. There would have been no other reason for the girl to be murdered. She was, after all, a slave who had nothing except a piece of information. Only someone who had been trained at covering their tracks would have taken such a calculated risk. He also realized that during wartime, there was always the possibility of espionage. This seemed highly plausible to him. He couldn't help but lean toward the belief that his suspect was a spy for the Union army, inserted into the city to gather information.

After putting on his uniform and washing his face, Thomas left his room and descended the stairs of the converted cotton warehouse. The walk from the barracks to his office would give him time to think about what he should do next. He knew presenting his spy theory to the colonel would do no good. The man probably wouldn't believe him, declaring his city was too secure to allow entrance to such a villain. In fact, he thought about not telling him at all. He contemplated downplaying the slave's murder and Chase's assault as a mere coincidence—a kind of "wrong place at the wrong time" situation. But he realized he couldn't do that. He had already lived with the lie about being wounded pursuing the enemy in battle, and it ate at him day after day. He would tell the truth, he decided, and see what happened from there.

Thomas entered the provost building and saluted the sentry. He walked past his office to the stairwell where he ascended to the second floor. He knocked on the colonel's door.

"Come in!" the colonel called from inside.

Thomas opened the door to find the colonel sitting at his desk. Above him, a cloud of white cigar smoke lingered a few feet from the ceiling. "Good morning, sir," Thomas greeted. "I have some information about the investigation."

The colonel stubbed out his cigar and closed a ledger on his desk. "What is it, Altman?"

"The witness I told you about was murdered last night," Thomas advised, walking closer to the colonel.

"Sit down," the colonel ordered. "Tell me what you know so far."

Thomas took a seat. "Lieutenant Chase was injured as well, sir. The same assailant who killed the witness attacked him. He's still unconscious."

Thomas noticed the colonel didn't seem surprised as he struck a match and lit a new cigar. "So, you think the man who murdered your witness and assaulted Lieutenant Chase also murdered the courier?"

"I do, sir."

The colonel stood up and walked to the window. He looked out with his back turned before replying, "Then this is a serious situation, Captain. Wouldn't you agree?" The colonel turned back around abruptly awaiting a reply.

Thomas was prepared to deliver his theory. "I do, sir. I believe we may be dealing with a spy."

The colonel didn't respond immediately. He paced back and forth in the small space behind his desk for a moment.

"If it is a spy, shouldn't we notify the general, sir?" Thomas asked.

The question broke the colonel from of his trance. "Absolutely not, Captain. I'm afraid that would cause a hysteria among the high command. This office will handle this investigation quietly and without asking for aid from anyone else. We will capture this, *whatever he is,* completely ourselves."

Thomas knew what the colonel was doing. His commander wanted all the glory of catching the spy for himself. "Very good, sir. What are your orders?"

The colonel put his cigar on the tip of the ashtray and placed both hands on the desk. His gray eyes focused squarely on Thomas. "I want you to find this man, Captain. Work day and night if you have to."

So that was it. Thomas was getting no help nor guidance from his commanding officer. He would have to go it alone to find the spy. "I'll do my best, sir," was all Thomas could say.

The colonel leaned off the desk and sat down in his chair. "You may take anyone you wish as your aide until Chase is recovered. Just make sure it's someone we can trust. You're dismissed."

Thomas snapped a salute before leaving the office. He wasn't happy with how the conversation went.

The investigation would be left solely to him, because if it went wrong, the colonel would be able to say he had no knowledge of the affair.

Walking back down the stairs and past his office, he made it into the street. He knew the only way to get any information was to use the small amount of evidence he had. And it wasn't much. Just a pipe and some spent tobacco, but it was better than nothing. The pipe was made of briar wood and had a small engraving of a Fleur de Lis on the bottom of the bowl. Other than this marking, there was nothing different about this pipe from any other. The tobacco was different though. What little bit was left would be valuable, because it wasn't South Carolina tobacco—it was Virginia grown. He knew this because he encountered the smell of it while he was with General Lee's army. And Virginia grown tobacco was hard to get in Charleston because of the Yankee blockade. He guessed it could only be found in one or two of the tobacco shops in the city. This would be a start. But that part of his investigation would wait. He had to see Inspector John James.

Thomas arrived at the police headquarters on St. Phillip Street. The inspector was exiting the building as he arrived. John was dressed in his usual attire: a dark brown suit, straw planter's hat, and shiny black shoes.

"Good morning, Captain. Heck of a night last night," John remarked.

Thomas was quick to agree, "To say the least, John. Do you have time to discuss the murder of Mr. Jones's servant?"

John slapped his shoulder. "Of course, I do. Let's walk."

They began to journey away from the police building. Although still aching from last night, Thomas was glad John hadn't invited him in to sit down. A leisurely walk sometimes made his knee feel better. "I believe this is more than just a murder," he said.

"How so?" John asked curiously.

"I'm not allowed to go into depth since it's a military matter, but let's just say I must find this man soon."

John shook his head. "I know you can't tell me everything, but can you answer one question?"

"If I can."

"Does this have to do with the murder of the courier?"

Thomas didn't realize John knew anything about the murder. "How do you know about that?"

"I'm with the police, Thomas. We try to know everything that goes on in the city, military or not," John answered, as the two stopped for a team of mules pulling artillery through the intersection.

Thomas didn't want to divulge too much military information; it wasn't allowed. But he knew his only chance at finding the murderer's identity was to ask for John's help. "I'm going to need your assistance on this one. We can investigate both murders simultaneously."

"Help each other, huh?" John replied, scratching his chin.

"I think it would be beneficial; I believe both cases have the same suspect," Thomas said.

"I don't see why not," John answered, the two stopping in front of a small tobacco shop. "Since we're working together now, I thought this may be a good place to start."

Thomas realized then that John was also following the tobacco lead. This was good. He was glad he could watch him at work now. He didn't have as much experience as the inspector and was more than willing to learn.

Upon entering, the fragrant aroma of tobacco leaf enveloped Thomas. Not one certain type, but many. They walked to the back where they found an elderly man behind the counter. He looked over his circle-shaped spectacles as they walked up.

"Can I help you, gentlemen?" the shopkeeper asked.

"I hope you can," John replied. "I'm with the police, and this captain is with the provost marshal."

A concerned look crossed the man's face. He quickly wiped his perspiring forehead with a white handkerchief he pulled from his pocket. "What have I done, sirs? I can assure you none of my product was obtained illegally."

"Let's hope not, sir," John answered. "Start by telling us your name."

"Louis Herring, sir."

"Very good, Louis. Just answer a few questions and we'll be on our way."

"I'll do my best," the shopkeeper replied, trying to force a smile.

"Do you sell any Virginia pipe tobacco?" John asked.

"I do, sir. Only the finest leaf is sold here."

Thomas took a paper pouch out of his pocket and opened it. It contained the tobacco found in the alley. "Do you have any of this type?" he asked Mr. Herring.

The shopkeeper took the pouch from Thomas's hand and placed it close to his nose. After a strong sniff, he gave the pouch back. "I do indeed sell this type, Captain. It's my most expensive brand. There aren't many men in the city who can afford to buy it. As you are aware, the blockade has made it difficult to procure any merchandise from outside the state."

"Would you be able to give us the names of the men you have sold it to?" John inquired.

Mr. Herring looked lost at the question but provided an answer nonetheless, "There are several officers from Virginia who purchase it, sir, but I'm sorry to say that I don't know their names."

Since Thomas believed the spy was masquerading as a common citizen and not a soldier, this eliminated any of the military customers Mr. Herring referred to. He had to narrow the possibilities. "How about any civilians?"

The shopkeeper raised his eyebrows. "Well, I do frequently sell it to one man. He's a tall gentleman with a pointed mustache. Doesn't say too much when he comes in. He left here shortly before you two arrived."

"Which way did he go?" John asked, his excitement showing.

"I didn't see, sir."

Thomas and John ran quickly to the door of the shop. They entered onto the street and looked in both directions, but the man Mr. Herring described was long gone.

Feeling deflated, Thomas walked back inside the shop, followed by John. He found Mr. Herring still behind the counter. "Here is my card," Thomas said, handing it over. "If you see this man again, please attempt to get a name. I can be found at the provost marshal's building."

"I will, sir," Mr. Herring replied, examining at the card.

As they left the shop, Thomas thought to ask John about what Mr. Jones said concerning his servant's death. He didn't speak to the prominent attorney last night, having been too focused on trying to save the life of

Lieutenant Chase. "What did Jones say about the murder, John?"

"He was surprised by the whole thing, to say the least. He had no idea she came by your office to see you. Her mother was the one who told her to go by our station to report what she saw. She must have been told to go to your place when she got there."

"Did she tell her mother what she witnessed?"

"Unfortunately, not," John replied, shaking his head.

This added to Thomas's already growing disappointment. His only hope now was that the man who purchased the tobacco would come back to the shop. Although it wouldn't mean this was the suspect, it could at least be someone of interest to question. Before he could ask John anything else, he saw her. Ellen Hiott was wearing a light gray dress with a matching hat, accompanied by a female Negro servant who was holding a basket.

"I'll come by and see you later. Let me know if you hear anything," Thomas said, unable to take his eyes off of her.

"Alright then," John replied, touching Thomas on the arm to get his attention. "You should come over for dinner tonight if you aren't busy. Margaret is a wonderful cook."

Thomas stopped staring at Ellen and turned to John, realizing he was being rude. "That would be real nice. Thank you for the invitation."

The two men shook hands before John disappeared into the city market crowd. Thomas crossed the street and made his way toward Ellen. Although John's dinner invitation was a kind gesture, Thomas would rather spend the evening with Ellen. He just hoped she would agree.

Chapter 10

Rhett left the tobacco shop and crossed the street to purchase a newspaper. As he was paying the vendor, he happened to look up and see the captain and the policeman from last night. They were entering the tobacco shop. Rhett walked into a haberdashery behind the newspaper stand in hopes of surveilling them for a moment.

"Good morning," an older gentleman in a black suit greeted. "Can I help you today?"

Rhett knew he needed to give a legitimate reason to be in the shop. "I'm looking for a brown necktie. Do you have any in stock?"

The shopkeeper nodded. "I do indeed, sir. Give me a moment while I retrieve one."

Rhett looked out of the front store window while the shopkeeper shuffled to the back. He saw both men exit the shop in a hurry, looking up and down the street. The tobacco shop owner must have given them his description.

"Here it is, sir," the shopkeeper said, returning from the rear of the store.

Rhett turned around and took the necktie from the man's hand. "This won't do; it's too light. Do you have anything darker?"

The shopkeeper retrieved the necktie. "I do, sir. One moment."

He returned to looking out the window. He saw the two men speaking to each other for a few minutes in front of the shop before heading off in different directions. He knew he needed to follow at least one of them.

Without waiting for the shopkeeper to return, he made his way into the busy street and began to follow the slower moving man—the limping captain. He followed him a short distance before stopping. Rhett saw him look over at a woman and her servant who were perusing flowers at a street vendor's stand. He watched as the captain approached her after running his hands through his brown hair and straightening his uniform. The two spoke briefly before the lady put her arm into his and the two began to walk. It was then he got a good look at the captain's acquaintance–it was Ellen Hiott. He was familiar with her since it was his employer's daughter. The bank president's only child would visit the bank on occasion to see her father, and he had been introduced to her when he first arrived in the city.

He followed the couple to Mr. Hiott's house a few blocks away. Once the two appeared to say their goodbyes, the captain left walking. Rhett continued his surveillance. He followed him to the provost marshal's office on Meeting Street. He was sure now that he was being investigated by both the police force and the provost marshal. This was not what he wanted.

"LaCroix!" a voice shouted, startling him.

Rhett looked over his shoulder to see Colonel Marlow atop his horse.

"We need to have a discussion. I'll meet you at your office in less than an hour," the colonel said, before snapping the reigns and riding away.

Rhett could tell the colonel wasn't happy. He guessed that his part-time employer was irritated with him for not performing any work on the accounts last night. Turning on his heels, he made a beeline for the bank. He was out longer than he should have been. The short break he was allotted each day had long been over. He didn't need any negative attention and hoped he wouldn't be reprimanded for being late.

Back at the bank, he walked into his office and closed the door. He needed time to think. His meeting with Hawkins last night did not go as he anticipated. The pat on the back he was expecting didn't happen, and the new task set before him was not only dangerous, it was difficult. Leaning back in his chair, he decided what to do next. He would have to eliminate the only other person who could identify him—the lieutenant he failed to kill last night. Once that was done, he would have to try and place himself above suspicion. The authorities might have some tobacco he smoked and his pipe, but that was not concrete evidence. He had been careful to cover his tracks other than that slip up, and he was confident he could talk his way out of anything. A knock on his door jarred him from his thoughts. He straightened his suit and answered the door. It was the colonel.

"Come in, sir, please have seat," Rhett offered, motioning for him to do so.

The colonel took off his gloves, placed them inside his hat, and sat the items on the corner of Rhett's desk. He took a seat in Rhett's chair.

"Close the door," the colonel ordered.

Rhett closed the door and took a seat in the client chair on the other side of the desk.

"I pay you to perform a very important duty," the colonel began, "and not doing as you're instructed causes me uneasiness about our arrangement. You did not do what I asked of you last night."

Rhett wanted to kill the man right there. A rebel colonel on his list of victims would surely make him feel more accomplished, but he knew he had to play the part. He had to maintain his cover for a little while longer. "I'm sorry, sir. I assure you it won't happen again."

The colonel leaned forward in the chair and folded his hands on the desk. His gray eyes were focused directly on Rhett. "Money is the most important thing to me, Rhett - and I become quite irritated when it's not looked after properly." The colonel paused for a moment but didn't break his stare. "You don't want me to become irritated, do you?"

Rhett dropped his head in an embarrassed manner. It was simply for show. "No, sir," he replied.

"Good," the colonel said. "I hope we won't need to have this uncomfortable conversation again."

"No, sir, we won't."

The colonel stood up to leave. Before making his way to the door, he stopped and looked at a still seated Rhett. "And by the way, be careful if you go out after hours. There have been two murders in as many nights."

"Thank you, sir," Rhett responded, watching the colonel leave.

He didn't move out of the chair for a few minutes. He reached into his pocket and took out his new pipe. This was a nicer one, given to him by his father. He didn't like carrying it around for fear he would lose it, but the incident last night left him no other option. He packed the pipe bowl, lit it, and began to smoke. Relaxed, he could think more clearly now. And with this clarity came a good idea. He jumped from his chair and walked to the end of the hall where he knocked on the last door.

"Come in," a voice said.

Rhett opened the door to find Mr. Hiott behind his desk, dusting a painting. The bank president's workspace was nothing short of elegant. It was a large room, filled with all the niceties only someone like Mr. Hiott could afford. There were several oriental rugs on the floor, which accented the two lush settees situated on the far wall.

"May I speak with you, sir?"

Mr. Hiott took a seat at his desk. "Absolutely, Rhett. What's on your mind?"

Rhett sat down and crossed his legs. "I wanted to thank you for the invitation to the ball last night. The event was one to be remembered."

Mr. Hiott smiled. "I knew you would enjoy it. Hopefully, you met some folks in need of our services."

"I hope I did, sir. I also wanted to compliment you on your home. It was quite immaculate."

"Thank you." Mr. Hiott paused to loosen his necktie and clear his throat. "You should visit again! Dinner tonight, perhaps?"

Rhett was hoping for the invitation, but he didn't expect it would be so soon. "Yes, that would be wonderful," he graciously replied.

After a few more minutes of small talk, he thanked Mr. Hiott again and left the office. He was anxious to leave the bank now. Knowing he would have to make it to the hospital to tie up a loose end before dinner tonight, he needed to hurry.

Rhett arrived at the barracks with his ever-present Bowie knife tucked into his trousers. The building was a large wooden structure on the bank of the Ashley River. The façade had the words, "Cotton Brokers," in large faded lettering above the main entrance. A sentry stood out-front clutching a musket. He knew he would have to give a good reason when asking permission to enter, as civilians were prohibited from most military buildings. "Good afternoon, soldier," Rhett greeted. "I'm looking for the military hospital."

The sentry looked at him suspiciously. "What's your business?" he asked stiffly.

"My cousin is an officer who was injured during the bombardment on Fort Sumter last night. His sister said he was brought here. I was told he may not have long, so I would like to see him as soon as possible." Rhett tried to look emotionally distraught while giving his false story.

"Through the main warehouse and all the way to the back. The last room is where the officers are tended to," the sentry responded.

"Thank you, soldier," Rhett replied tipping his hat.

As he neared the hospital portion of the building, he noticed a foul smell. The acrid scent of death hung heavy in the air. Putting his left arm's sleeve over his face to mask the odor, he entered the first warehouse. At least a hundred men were there. They were lying in dirty beds, covered by equally dirty sheets. One or two nurses seemed to be the only staff members assigned to care for the multitude of wounded. There were moans and pleas for help from the soldiers as he passed by, but he offered them no mind. He hated these rebels and hoped they would die.

Entering the second warehouse, the smell was a bit less overpowering. He knew the army did their best to look after the officers, as they believed a leader was much more valuable than a fighting man. He paused for a moment to look around for the lieutenant. Rhett remembered the young man's face well. He just had to find him.

"May I help you, sir?" a female nursed asked. She was red-haired and dressed in a white hospital apron.

He quickly came up with a clever lie since he didn't know the officer's name. "Yes, you may," he replied, smiling. "I'm with the army medical department. I've come for an inspection of the facility."

The nurse's eyes widened. She pushed her hair up and straightened her apron. "No one told us about an inspection, sir. I'll fetch the head surgeon to meet with you."

As she turned to leave, Rhett grabbed her arm. "No ma'am, that won't be necessary. This is an informal inspection." He leaned in close to the nurse and whispered, "This is an unannounced, secret inspection. We want to see how things are done when the medical staff aren't aware we're coming."

The nurse nodded and put her hand to her mouth. "I understand, sir," she whispered back.

"Very good, then. Can you please maintain this secret until I leave?"

"Yes, sir." The nurse bowed slightly and continued on with her day.

Rhett began to walk down the row of beds in search of his target. But as he neared the end of the first row, he didn't find the lieutenant. He turned around and checked the second row of beds. At the end of this pass, he had no luck. The lieutenant wasn't there. Feeling nervous and confused, he quickly made his way out of the officer's section and through the enlisted side. He tipped his hat to the sentry he had spoken to as he entered, the sentry nodding back. When he made it to the street, he was sweating, worried about what to do next. His life would be in grave danger should this lieutenant be able to identify him. He checked his watch and saw it was close to six o'clock. He slowed his walk to try and calm his nerves. Knowing he would now have to play the part of Rhett the loan officer, he would have to clear his mind of any concerns. With killing the lieutenant now out of the question, he decided he needed to move on to the other part of his plan. He realized that being a valued employee at the Bank of Charleston, and Colonel Marlow's secret bookkeeper, may have its benefits. He could use his connections to make his job easier and less dangerous. Or at least he hoped so.

Chapter 11

Thomas sat in his office peering over the notes he had taken so far concerning the courier murder. Although he had worked other murders before, this one was different. This killer was much more than a common criminal. A Union spy was trained to kill and trained to stay hidden. To make matters worse, he had no leads. His hopes on the tobacco evidence had been dashed earlier that day. But as he shuffled his paperwork around to different stacks, he remembered his plans for the evening. He was to have dinner with Ellen Hiott. Unexpectedly, Lieutenant Chase walked through the office door. Thomas, not expecting to see him, was elated. "Chase! What are you doing here?"

The lieutenant had his arm in a sling and his head was partially bandaged. A light bruise covered the right side of his face where the assailant struck him. "Good afternoon, sir," he greeted. His voice was noticeably hoarse.

Thomas stood up, shook his hand, and offered him a chair. "When were you discharged?" he asked.

"This morning, sir," Chase answered, sitting down. "The surgeons said I should try and rest as much as possible. I'm told the arm should be healed well enough to return in a day or so." Chase cringed before using his good arm to rub the back of his head. "I would, however, feel much better if this headache would go away."

"You took a hard hit," Thomas said. "You're lucky to be alive."

"I know, sir."

He didn't want to seem pushy about asking Chase if he had seen the man's face, but Thomas knew the question couldn't wait. "Did you get a look at the assailant?"

Chase dropped his head and shook it slowly from side to side. "Unfortunately, no. I don't remember much of anything, sir."

Thomas felt disheartened yet again. Chase couldn't identify the man. He had to move on. "No worries, Chase," he assured. "We'll get our hands on him soon enough. Now I want you to get back and get some rest. That's an order."

Thomas waited for the lieutenant to leave before making his way out as well. He needed to get back to the barracks to prepare for dinner tonight.

Once back in his room, he changed into his best uniform. Unfortunately, his best uniform wasn't impressive. The shortage of cloth in the city had made the purchase of any new uniforms nearly impossible. He ran a comb through his hair and put on his white dress gloves.

Satisfied that he looked as presentable as he possibly could, he left his room and began the walk to the Hiott house. He had planned to take Ellen to a French restaurant in the city market. Although the cost of a meal there would sap his finances for a week or so, he felt the need to make a good impression.

Thomas arrived shortly after six o'clock. He knocked on the door. It was soon answered by the same servant he had seen the night of the ball.

"Evening, sir. You're Captain Altman?" he asked.

"I am."

"Come in please."

Thomas entered the foyer and removed his hat. The servant took it and placed it behind his stand.

"I'll let Mr. Hiott know you've arrived," the servant advised.

When Thomas sat down, he heard voices. They weren't far off. He could tell the people conversing were not pleased with each other. A few moments later, Ellen entered the hallway. She had changed into a more elegant dress than she was wearing at the market today. She was beautiful. His heart beat faster simply at her sight.

"Good evening, Captain," she greeted, smiling. The servant was a few steps behind her.

"Good evening," Thomas replied in kind. "Are you ready to leave?"

Ellen's smile faded as she looked down at the floor. "I can't leave tonight."

Thomas didn't know what to say. He looked back at her blankly.

"My father has instructed me that I must stay here for dinner. He has offered you an invitation as well," she said, now meeting his curious gaze.

He could tell by the way she was acting that she didn't want to stay. But he knew an unmarried woman living in her father's home had no choice but to follow instructions. "I'd be honored to dine here," he said, trying to sound grateful for the invitation.

She reached for his hand. "Then please come this way."

The two walked past the ballroom and into the dining room. Mr. Hiott and another man rose from the table upon their entry. He immediately remembered the guest to be the one he saw here before, the nervous man with the pointed mustache. Thomas stood beside Ellen in the doorway and watched as both men approached him.

Mr. Hiott shook Thomas's hand first. "I'm glad you accepted my invitation, Captain. My daughter neglected to tell me she had plans tonight," he said, casting a cold glance in her direction.

"Thank you for the invitation, sir. As I told Ellen, I would be honored to attend."

Mr. Hiott nodded at Thomas and made his way back to the table. Next, the guest introduced himself. "My name is Rhett LaCroix," he said, offering a handshake to Thomas. "Pleased to meet you."

Thomas couldn't tell for sure what it was, but something about this man seemed strange. It was a gut feeling, but that's all it was. The two broke off their handshake and he shook off the vibe. "Pleased to meet you, Mr. LaCroix."

"Trust me, Captain," Lacroix replied, "the pleasure is all mine."

Chapter 12

Rhett sat down at the table beside his employer. He came here expecting to gain information on the identity of the captain who was looking for leads at the tobacco shop today. But this, he did not expect. His pursuer sat directly across from him, apparently unaware of his identity. He hoped-for his sake-to find out if any headway had been made in the investigation. He particularly wanted to learn if the lieutenant he tried to kill was able to give a description of him.

"A toast to our fighting men defending the city," Mr. Hiott said, lifting his glass.

Rhett, the captain, and Ellen lifted their glasses. Everyone drank the toast and returned the fine crystal chalices to the table. Rhett waited on Mr. Hiott to begin eating before starting any conversation.

"So, Captain," Rhett began, "I'm told you work with the provost marshal."

"I do, sir," the captain replied.

"Are you currently conducting any interesting investigations?"

The captain put his fork down and looked up at Rhett. He slowly wiped his mouth with his napkin before answering, "I'm not at liberty to discuss current investigations, Mr. LaCroix. I'm sure you understand."

"I understand perfectly, Captain. I apologize if I asked something I shouldn't have," Rhett responded in a respectful tone. "But when I heard about the incident at Randall Jones's home, I must admit I was a little disturbed."

Mr. Hiott put his fork down and stared across the table. Rhett knew talking about the Jones incident would strike a chord.

"I'm very distressed about that too, Captain," Mr. Hiott interjected. "Mr. Jones is an important man in this city."

The captain looked at Mr. Hiott. Rhett could tell he was being forced by the powerful banker to give some sort of information on the crime, and that was what he hoped for.

"It's distressing indeed, sir," the captain answered. "But I can discuss what I know about that matter since the victim was a civilian. Police Inspector James is handling that investigation."

Rhett tried to appear calm, but he was nervous. He feared what was going to come out of the captain's mouth next.

"I've been told the police have no leads in the servant's murder, "the captain advised. "The mother of the victim was unable to identify her assailant."

This answer seemed to satisfy Mr. Hiott who nodded and returned to eating. It wasn't good enough for Rhett though. He needed to know about the lieutenant.

"I hope the police will find the bandit," Rhett said, sounding mildly concerned. "Something has to be done before any more of our citizens lose their lives."

"I do as well," the captain replied.

A few minutes passed. Rhett began to converse with Mr. Hiott about bank matters while Ellen spoke to the captain. Anxious to pry more information from Captain Altman, Rhett waited until there was a break in the conversation between himself and Mr. Hiott. When his employer took another bite, he took the opportunity. "Have you any help in your duties, Captain? It would seem you aren't the only one handling the matters of the provost." He could tell the captain was slightly annoyed that he disrupted his conversation with Ellen.

The captain answered, "I'm usually aided by a lieutenant. Unfortunately, though, he will be on bedrest for a while.

"I'm sorry to hear that. Was he injured by an enemy shell?"

"No," the captain responded flatly.

Rhett knew when to stop. Feeling satisfied the lieutenant knew nothing of his identity, he picked up his glass and took a slow sip of his brandy. He was feeling confident that he was in the clear.

Ellen spoke up, "May we go on a walk, Father? I need some fresh air."

"Yes, but be careful," he replied cautiously. "This city is becoming more dangerous than ever, I'm afraid."

Rhett watched on as the captain thanked Mr. Hiott for dinner. Being formal, he walked around the table to bid the captain farewell. "Thank you for the conversation this evening, Captain," Rhett said as the two shook hands. "Should you have any financial needs, please see me at the bank."

"Thank you, Mr. LaCroix."

Rhett remained standing in the dining room while the two departed. Mr. Hiott came over and touched him on the shoulder, grabbing his attention. "What do you think of him, Rhett? Is he the type of gentleman I want courting my daughter?"

Rhett turned to him and grinned. "I believe he is indeed, sir. Any criminal he pursues will have to work hard to stay ahead of him."

"He appears intelligent to you?" Mr. Hiott asked.

"Very intelligent, sir. Very intelligent."

Chapter 13

Thomas sat at his desk unable to focus. He was in an excellent mood after the stroll last night with Ellen. He couldn't stop thinking about her. Completely drawn to her in every way, he was hopeful they would be able to see each other again. He knew Mr. Hiott would not have allowed his daughter to court anyone like him if there wasn't a war on. Being a low-ranking officer who had little means to support a woman of Ellen's status, he would have been turned away at the front door. The war had changed things though. Many of the usual suitors were either off fighting in some distant theater or already dead. This being the case, he liked his chances of a prolonged relationship.

He took a deep breath. Knowing he needed to work on the investigation, he picked up his pen and looked at the sheet of paper sitting in front of him. But Thomas had nothing to write. He was at a standstill. No new leads had developed, and Lieutenant Chase's inability to give a description of his assailant proved to be a serious blow. He did, however, have a suspicion. He felt Mr. LaCroix fit the description of the man who bought the Virginia tobacco from Mr. Herring's shop. The chances of the spy being LaCroix were slim-he knew this; but there was something about him. It was a gut feeling. He didn't have any other leads anyway, and there could be little harm in at least getting to know the man better. He put his pen back down in the inkwell and reached for his hat. He was going respond to the loan officer's invitation.

When Thomas arrived at the bank, he noticed his knee wasn't as achy as usual. He surmised the good night's sleep he acquired must have temporarily eased the pain.

"May I help you, sir?" a young teller asked Thomas as he made it to the counter. The older man, in his fifties, looked eager to help. He lifted his pen awaiting a response.

"Yes, you may," Thomas answered, beginning to remove his gloves. "I'm looking for Mr. LaCroix."

The teller put his pen down and took a quick glance behind him. "I believe he's in his office, sir. Give me a moment to check. May I ask your name?"

"Captain Altman."

"Thank you, sir. I'll be back in a moment."

Thomas watched as the man moved into a hallway and out of sight. It was no less than a few minutes when he heard a door open and saw LaCroix approaching him from across the lobby.   "Captain Altman," LaCroix said, smiling broadly. He was dressed in a dark black suit that seemed to match the color of his hair and mustache. He walked over and the two shook hands.

"Is the invitation to visit still extended, Mr. LaCroix?" Thomas asked.

"Please call me Rhett. And yes, it is. Accompany me to my office."

Thomas followed LaCroix through a door behind the teller windows. A short walk brought him to a green door which LaCroix opened, allowing Thomas in first. It was then he noticed the smell. The sweet aroma of pipe tobacco filled the space. He brushed it aside as a coincidence, hoping to stay objective. To jump to any conclusions now would be ill-advised.

"Please have a seat, Captain," LaCroix offered. "Have you a financial matter that I can help you with?"

Thomas sat in the client chair in front of the desk and put his hat and gloves in his lap. "No, sir. I have another matter to discuss with you."

LaCroix looked confused for a moment. "What could that be?" he asked curiously.

"I've come. . ." Thomas was interrupted.

"Wait-before you begin, would you mind if I smoked while we talked?" LaCroix asked.

"Not at all," Thomas answered with a short wave of his hand. "It's your office, sir."

LaCroix stood up and opened the window behind him. Thomas could hear the voices of the citizens on the street outside. He then watched as the banker sat back down, packed his pipe with tobacco, and lit it with a match. The white puff of smoke from his first draw rolled out of the window like a cloud being pushed by the wind.

"That's better. Now let's talk, Captain. You were saying?"

"I've come to ask you some questions, Mr. LaCroix."

"Call me Rhett, I insist," LaCroix corrected him.

"Very well, *Rhett*," Thomas said slowly, putting an emphasis on the name. "I've been looking into the murder of a soldier that occurred two nights ago."

Rhett nodded and stared at Thomas, his lips wrapped tightly around the pipe.

"During the course of my investigation," Thomas continued, "I've learned the suspect smokes a certain type of tobacco. It's Virginia grown. Somewhat difficult to acquire here."

Thomas was focused on the man's eyes. He was looking for any shakiness, any signs of nervousness, but he saw none.

Slowly, LaCroix took the pipe out of his mouth and blew a cloud of smoke to the ceiling. "I smoke Virginia tobacco, Captain. I find it's much smoother than the Deep South type. Unfortunately, I've only been able to locate it in one shop. The name of the man who runs it is Herring, I believe. It's a small place in the city market."

Thomas's suspicions began to wane. After all, just because LaCroix smoked the same tobacco as the murderer meant nothing. But he still had a feeling that something wasn't right. He didn't know why he felt that way, he just did. He pressed on, "Yes, I've been to Mr. Herring's place."

LaCroix leaned on the desk and folded his hands. His facial expression changed now. He looked confused. "Forgive me if I sound rude, but why have you come here?"

"Just for the conversation, nothing more," Thomas replied calmly.

"Well, that's good to hear. I thought for a moment I was being implicated in some sort of crime," LaCroix said, the smile now returning to his face. "Should you need a loan though, I'd be happy to help with that."

"I'm afraid I haven't the need to inquire about a loan. Perhaps once the war is over."

"And do you think the South will defeat the North, Captain?" LaCroix asked randomly.

Thomas thought it an odd question. Call it arrogance or pride, the people of Charleston had no doubt the Confederate Army would triumph over the Yankees. "I do, sir," he replied. "The Confederacy's fighting men believe in their cause. The men of the northern army only fight because they're paid to do so."

After answering, LaCroix stared at him for a moment. It was a strange silence—a silence that made Thomas feel uneasy. He pushed on, hoping a little more conversation may help him confirm or disprove any suspicions. "You aren't from here," Thomas implied. "I'm guessing from your accent that you come from Louisiana."

LaCroix gave a sly grin as he took another toke of the pipe. "Very astute, sir. I'm from New Orleans, born and raised."

"What part of New Orleans?" Thomas asked.

"The French Quarter."

"I've been there once," Thomas said. "I stayed at a hotel on Rue Bourbon, right on the Mississippi. I could see the steamers from my room window."

LaCroix nodded his head in acknowledgment. "Yes, I know Rue Bourbon well. Beautiful views of the river from there."

There was a pause in the conversation, and Thomas felt the time was right to leave. He stood up and put on his hat and gloves. "Thank you for the conversation, Rhett, but I must attend to my duties now."

LaCroix stood up as well. "Come back anytime, Captain. My offer of financial assistance to you remains extended."

"Thank you."

The two men shook hands before Thomas exited the smoky office. He turned to look back as he entered the lobby. LaCroix was in his office doorway staring at him. It was easy to tell the look was not one of kindness.

He crossed back over the shiny floor and walked out into the Charleston sunshine. Donning his gray kepi, he started north to his office. He began to think his talk with LaCroix had gone better than he could have hoped for. Although LaCroix said nothing to incriminate himself, Thomas learned something about the man today—he was a liar. Thomas had been to New Orleans while he was a cadet at The Citadel. His classmate was a fiery creole whose family owned a hotel in the French Quarter. While on that trip, he toured Bourbon Street, or Rue Bourbon, as the French called it. It ran east to west a few blocks north of the river, clearly out of view of the mighty waterway. Any New Orleans resident should have known that. But interestingly, Rhett LaCroix did not.

Chapter 14

Rhett assumed Marlow would be waiting for him. The colonel would want to make sure he showed up after the warning. But this was what he wanted. He would no longer have to worry about anyone investigating him after tonight.

Taking his usual way up to the office, he lurked about in the stairwell for a moment to make sure the hallway was empty. Satisfied, he opened the door and made his way across the creaky floor to the colonel's office. He tried the doorknob before using his key—it was unlocked. He slowly entered to find the colonel at his desk.

"I have plenty of work for you to do," the colonel said, watching Rhett walk in.

Rhett closed the door behind him and put his top hat on a hook by the door. "I assure you I can handle it, sir."

The colonel stood up and pointed to a large stack of papers on the desk. "I need you to make sure the captains of the blockade runners receive compensation for their services. Use my personal account at your bank to pay them."

"Yes, sir."

Marlow came from the behind the desk and headed for the door. He turned around just before leaving. "Your compensation is in the drawer. Please get everything done by the morning."

"Yes, sir," Rhett replied, raising his finger in a gesture to wait. "Before you leave, Colonel, may I speak with you briefly about a disturbing matter?"

Marlow took his hand off the doorknob and turned to Rhett. He looked inconvenienced by the question. "What is it?"

Rhett moved closer to him, finger tapping on his chin. "I had a visitor from your office today. A Captain Thomas Altman."

The colonel folded his arms across his chest and peered at Rhett. "Why did he come see you?"

"It's rather embarrassing, sir."

"I don't care, let's have it."

Rhett let out a short laugh. "I am apparently a suspect in the murder of some soldier. I believe he said it was a courier or something."

"Altman said that?"

"Indirectly, sir. He said I smoke the same tobacco as the man who killed this soldier."

The colonel unfolded his arms hastily and opened the door. "I'll handle that, son. You just do what you do best. Keep the ledger straight."

Marlow disappeared into the hallway. Rhett could hear the colonel's footsteps were heavier than usual, as if angrily stomping to the staircase. *That will work nicely,* he thought. He took off his coat and placed it on the back of the colonel's chair before sitting down. As usual, he looked in the desk drawers for any military correspondence that might benefit him, but to his dismay, there was nothing new. Just a few letters detailing suspicious activities about the city. Picking up the documents left for him, he found several promissory notes from cotton brokers in Liverpool detailing the amounts to be paid to the colonel for three black-market shipments. Marlow had used his authority as provost marshal to seize goods, especially cotton, which he quickly sold for a sizeable profit. Rhett's primary job was to keep the finances of this small empire appearing legitimate and making sure certain money transfers took place. Having performed these duties well, he believed he was indispensable to the colonel, which now proved to be an important thing, because he needed the colonel to order his subordinate, Captain Altman, to cease his investigation immediately.

Rhett finished his work just before ten o'clock. He opened the desk drawer and took the small pouch of gold coins that was left for him. The colonel knew Confederate money was becoming less valuable by the day; therefore, Rhett was paid in the only currency that always remained stable.

He took his hat and made his way out of the building. He was far more relaxed than he had been in the past few days. He knew the colonel would take care of his little problem, allowing him to operate unmolested. Feeling the urge to celebrate this small victory, he decided to spend one or two of his coins at one of the local taverns. But he also needed something important to his mission, and a tavern was the best place to acquire it.

He stopped at an establishment a few blocks away named *The Palmetto*. It was one of the classier establishments on the peninsula, serving several different types of whiskey and wine. Rhett had been here many times before, trying to listen to conversations between the sometimes loose-lipped Confederate officers. Alcohol had a way of making these men tell their secrets, and he was always ready to capitalize on that foolishness. The place was busy tonight, nearly full. Rhett made his way over to the bar. The tavern keeper stood there watching him approach.

"What's your drink?" the tavern keeper asked.

"Whiskey, please."

The man poured a single cup, but Rhett wanted more. "Leave the bottle."

"That's going to cost you," the tavern keeper spat.

Rhett reached into the pouch and took out two of the gold coins. He tossed the shiny objects on the bar. They bounced twice before resting flat. "No gray backs here. I'll pay you in real money."

The tavern keeper's eyes widened at the sight. "I believe this will cover it," he said, taking the coins and sliding them quickly into his pocket.

Rhett took the bottle to a corner table and lit his pipe. As he smoked, he began to screen the room for a victim. He saw a middle-aged officer sitting at table nearby. The man looked half-drunk and was about his height and weight—which was important. A single star sewn on the collar showed he possessed the rank of major. Rhett rose from the table and approached the officer who was staring into his empty cup. "Good evening, Major. May I join you?"

The major looked up at Rhett with a suspicious gaze. "Why?" he half slurred.

"I've found a little conversation makes the time here more enjoyable. Wouldn't you agree?"

"Fine," the major said, gesturing to the empty chair across from him.

Rhett sat down, putting his cup and whiskey bottle on the table. He knew what needed to happen for him to achieve his objective, so he got right down to business. "Major, allow me to pour you a drink. I always try to show the fighting men how much I appreciate their sacrifice to protect our freedom."

A small, reluctant smile appeared on the major's face. "Pour away then."

Rhett knew money was slim amongst the soldiers in the city, and any of them would appreciate a glass of free spirits. He filled the man's cup. "Your name, Major?"

"Billy Sanford," he said, before quickly downing the whiskey.

"The pleasure is all mine, Major. I'm Henri DuBois, a cotton broker from Biloxi." Rhett lied, knowing he couldn't give his real name.

Rhett poured the officer another drink and the two began to converse. He learned that Major Sanford was from Alabama, and that he was stationed at Fort Wagner. Rhett wasn't trying to gather any information tonight about military matters, but this was a bonus. As he drank more, the major told him about the set-up of the fort and the armaments it contained. Rhett made sure not to drink as fast as his new acquaintance. He wanted to be sure he could remember this useful information.

As Major Sanford was having to close one eye to focus now, Rhett knew the time was right to make his move. "Let us leave this place, Major. I suggest we head to another establishment to continue our conversation."

"That sounds splendid, sir," the major replied, wobbling to his feet. He stumbled as he tried to put on his hat, having to place one hand on the wall to stay upright.

It was late in the Holy City- almost midnight-when Rhett helped Major Sanford out of the tavern. The streets were still teeming with soldiers and civilians looking for a good time in the establishments that lined this part of King Street. The two men continued to chat as Rhett assisted the major's walking. But that wouldn't last long. Seeing a space between two buildings, Rhett steered the major into the alley under the auspice of relieving himself. The major just shook his head without replying, for he had started to sing the song *Dixie* loudly and off-key. Rhett leaned the major on the wall inside the alley and stepped a few paces back. He thought about pulling his knife. The desire to kill another rebel burned hotly within him, but he decided against it. Reaching down for a rock by his foot, he picked it up, and squeezed it tightly in his right hand. The major was still singing the song, unaware of what Rhett was doing. Pulling his arm back, Rhett delivered a blow that landed squarely on the left side of the major's face. The major fell to the ground instantly. Rhett walked to the edge of the alley and looked around, seeing no one. He moved back and began to undress the now unconscious soldier. He took all the garments, including the major's hat and Remington revolver.

Rhett made his way back into the street with the newly acquired items tucked under his arm. He was in a good mood now and was happy he hadn't killed the man. It would have been easy though. One swift swipe of his Bowie would have done it, but the murder of a higher-ranking officer would cause a frenzy among the military authorities, and his activities needed no more attention. He instead decided to chance that the major would awaken from his slumber and not report the matter. Doing so would be to admit that he engaged in conduct unbecoming of an officer. *No,* Rhett thought, *he won't tell anyone about this.* But his main concern now was getting back to his room. To be found on the street with these items in his possession would surely lead to his arrest.

Within a block the tailor shop, he felt the presence of someone behind him. A quick look over his shoulder confirmed his suspicion that he was being followed. The figure was close, maybe thirty feet away. Seeing a vacant lot, with a few shrubby trees on his left, he planned to enter it to see if the figure continued to follow. He turned into the space casually, put down his newly acquired items, and pulled his knife. The person followed him in. Rhett leaped from the darkness and swung his knife at his follower. The man parried the move with surprising speed and knocked him to the ground.

"Easy, LaCroix," a familiar voice ordered.

It was Hawkins.

Rhett remained on the ground, embarrassed. He would have been dead if it had been a rebel agent. "Why are you following me?" he asked, getting to his feet and dusting off his trousers. "I told you there was no need for that."

"I could care less what you say," Hawkins retorted.

"As you can see," Rhett said, pointing over to the stolen uniform, "I'm taking steps that will help me complete my mission."

Hawkins shrugged. "That wasn't what I was coming to see you about."

"Then what's the reason for this?"

"That captain," Hawkins began, "the one that met you at the bank. He's with the provost marshal, yes?"

Rhett couldn't believe what he was hearing. "How did you know about that?"

"Don't concern yourself with how I know. I just want to be sure he isn't on to you."

Rhett remained quiet. He didn't want to lie, but he didn't want to tell the truth either.

"Ah, I see by your silence that you may have given yourself away."

"I didn't give myself away," Rhett replied confidently. "But I can assure you the captain will be concerned with me no more."

"How can you be sure? Is he dead?"

"No," Rhett began, "but I've taken other steps. I've already had to assault one rebel officer and I don't need any more attention."

"That may be so," Hawkins mused. "After all, it's your funeral if you're wrong."

"Anything else?" Rhett asked. He was becoming irritated.

Hawkins moved into a sliver of light emanating from a home's nearby window. The long, broad scar on his face gave him a devious look. "Just help the troops get into Wagner. That's all."

Rhett didn't answer. He picked up the stolen items and left. Nothing more needed to be said.

Chapter 15

Thomas checked on Lieutenant Chase at the barracks before heading out for the night. The lieutenant said he was feeling better now and asked to return to duty. Thomas politely refused the request, telling Chase he had to obey the physician's wishes. He wanted the lieutenant back badly, especially since he now believed Rhett LaCroix was their suspect. But Chase's health was paramount to any investigation, and he knew the lieutenant needed to fully recover.

When he finally made it to the Hiott house, Thomas was brimming with excitement. Ellen had accepted his invitation for a late evening walk near the harbor. He knocked twice on the door with his left hand; his right contained a red rose he had purchased from a shop on the way over. He hoped she would find the gesture romantic, and not silly. The front door opened slowly, and the usual servant appeared. "Good evening, Captain. Miss Hiott is on her way down. Please come in."

Ellen appeared at the doorway before Thomas could make it inside. "Thank you, William. Tell Father I'll be back shortly."

The servant nodded and closed the door. Ellen and Thomas were left alone on the steps. He said nothing before presenting her the rose. He was nervous.

She smiled as she took the flower, which was the sign he needed to let him know his gesture was well received. "You don't have to shower me with gifts, Thomas. Your company is all I require."

He didn't say anything for a moment, he just looked at her. Although she wasn't dressed in her formal attire, she was still breathtaking. "I know you don't need the rose, but I felt I should bring you something," he said. "I was hoping we could walk by the harbor. It's quite nice when the guns are silent."

"I haven't been down there in some time. Father tells me it is too dangerous with the Yankee gunboats prowling about," she replied.

"The Yankee boats can't make it close enough to fire on the peninsula. They haven't been able to make it past Sumter so far," he assured her. "Trust me when I tell you that you're completely safe."

They talked about a myriad of topics ranging from popular books to the weather during their walk. Thomas enjoyed the conversation immensely. The war had caused him to focus entirely on his duties, giving him no time to consider relationships of any type. The time he was now spending with Ellen made him realize just how empty his life had been.

"What were your duties prior to being assigned here?" Ellen inquired, the two coming within sight of the harbor.

Thomas didn't know if he should tell her the truth. Although a lie, he would give her the same account that he had given the general. The admission of being a coward, he knew, would do nothing to help him win her heart. "I fought at the Battle of Sharpsburg in Maryland last year. Have you heard of it?"

Ellen shook her head slightly. "I know of it. Everyone has said the field was laden with bodies afterwards. I've been told it was a horrible defeat."

"It was horrible," Thomas agreed. "I was injured there and sent back to recuperate. After I was well, I was assigned to work with the provost marshal. To be honest, I'm glad I didn't get shipped back to Virginia."

The two stopped at the wharf near the South Battery. The Union blockade had caused a stockpile of vessels to be moored here and every available slip was occupied. The appearance of idle ships was in stark contrast to the busy wharf of two years ago.

"It's beautiful here," Ellen observed, staring out into the water. "I don't know why my mother was so eager to leave a place as nice as this."

Thomas remembered Ellen mentioning this when he first met her. He believed the comment to be an invitation to inquire about it further. "Your mother isn't here in the city?"

"No. She left for Europe when the war started. She told my father she couldn't bear to be besieged by the Yankees."

"You haven't seen her in two years?" Thomas asked.

"I haven't. But our relationship wasn't the best anyway. I wonder if she even misses me."

"Will she return after the war?"

Ellen shook her head. "Probably not. She was born in Scotland and always wanted to go back. The war was a good excuse to get what she wanted."

"But you stayed?"

"I couldn't leave Father by himself. He would have been devastated to see both of us go."

"That's admirable," Thomas replied. "It would have been easy for you to leave this situation. The war has been hard on the people here."

Ellen turned to him and put her hands on his chest. "It has," she replied, looking into his eyes. "But If I had left, I wouldn't have met you."

They kissed. He didn't expect it. He held her tightly. Ellen did the same, not pushing him away, but holding him tighter. They were interrupted by a sudden, loud sound. Thomas looked up quickly to see a flare high in the sky, its bright glow illuminating a Union ironclad ship slowly approaching Fort Sumter. He watched on as several more flares were fired, revealing two more ironclads, three in all. He grabbed Ellen's hand and ran for the street.

"What's happening?" Ellen yelled, as she was being pulled up the dock by Thomas.

"Just follow me!" he shouted back.

The guns began to fire now. All the forts and batteries around the harbor were opening up on the three gunboats.

They made it a block to the South Battery. It was a small fortress, just enough for three cannons. It also contained a bombproof shelter where Thomas knew Ellen would be safe.

Upon entering the battery, it was a hotbed of activity. Soldiers ran in every direction, officers were shouting orders, cannons were being fired. He led Ellen to the shelter at the center of the bastion. It was a brick building with sandbags lining the roof. Once safe inside, he sat her down. "Stay here," he told her. "I'll be back once the shooting stops."

"I'll be fine. Go," Ellen ordered.

Heading outside to find the battery commander, the sounds of war filled the night air. His heart raced with both excitement and worry. With those feelings colliding with each other, he began to wonder if he would shy away from the danger—flee like before. But he was determined to redeem himself. Or so he hoped.

Reaching the command post, he heard the distinct whistle of an incoming shell. The sound was not foreign to him. The soldiers nearby instinctively hit the ground waiting for the impact, including Thomas. The shell struck the side of the shelter Ellen was taking refuge in. Shrapnel and dirt flew hundreds of feet into the air. The unfortunate men who found themselves close to the explosion were sent tumbling skyward like rag dolls. Not waiting for the smoke to clear, Thomas leaped to his feet and raced to find Ellen. He prayed she was still alive. To lose her like this would be unimaginable. He found the roof partially caved in, blocking the entrance. He pulled the rubble from the doorway frantically, not noticing that several soldiers had joined to help after seeing his struggle. Then he saw her. She was sitting on the ground holding her knees with both arms, rocking from side to side. She looked terrified. He moved in, grabbed her, and held her tight. He looked down to see she was bleeding from her shoulder.

"You've been hit?" he asked.

Ellen didn't respond. She was catatonic.

"Ellen!" he shouted, turning her head so he could stare into her eyes.

"Yes, but I'm fine!" she finally cried, coming around. "Are you?"

"I am. Let's get you out of here," Thomas replied, lifting her to her feet.

The fight had stopped as quickly as it had begun. The three ironclads made their way past Fort Sumter before being turned away by the batteries on the peninsula. All was quiet now, except for the screams of the wounded men that littered the ground.

Realizing it was now safe, he led Ellen out of the battery. He still couldn't believe what happened. He thought the bombproof would have been the safest place for her, but he had been wrong. He tried to see how severe the wound to her shoulder was, but it was too dark. He walked to a nearby building where he pulled a lantern from the door. He held it close enough to see a tear in Ellen's shirt, and beneath it, a bloody gash.

"Can you move your arm?" he asked.

Ellen was crying now. "Yes, but it hurts."

Thomas ripped her good shirtsleeve off and twisted it to form a makeshift bandage. He wrapped it tightly around the wound to try and stop the bleeding.

"I don't think it's serious, but we need to get you back home," he said.

He saw an open buggy approaching them being pulled by two horses. Thomas stepped out into the street and waved the lantern, so he could be seen by the driver at the reigns. The buggy stopped abruptly.

The Negro driver tipped his hat to Thomas but eyed him suspiciously. "Help you, sir?" he asked.

"This is Calvin Hiott's daughter, and she's been injured. Is there any way you can take us to her house on Meeting Street?" Thomas tried to sound calm, but he knew his voice sounded nervous.

"Yessir. Get on in," the driver said.

He was glad he didn't have to commandeer the buggy. He would have done so if the man refused his request. All that mattered was getting Ellen back home. Helping her up into the seat, he patted the driver on the shoulder. "Drive on."

The driver snapped the reigns and headed north. Thomas was mad at himself for taking her down to the harbor. They could have stayed close to her house tonight, but he wanted to treat her to a nice view. That had been a horrible mistake. He was also concerned how this would be received by her father.

After a few minutes of riding through the city's bumpy streets, they stopped in front of the Hiott house. Thomas gave the driver a five dollar note and thanked him for the ride. He looked at Ellen's arm to see it had all but stopped bleeding, but he could tell she was still immensely disturbed by the ordeal. Forgoing the knock on the front door, he turned the knob and the two entered. He found the house servant approaching him. The man's mouth dropped when he was close enough to see the wound on Ellen's arm.

"Miss Ellen, what happened?" he said, putting his arm around her.

"A shell from a gunboat fell near us," Thomas replied. "I didn't think they would be able to get that close."

"I'll take her to her room and notify Mr. Hiott of what's happened. I'm sure he will want to speak to you, Captain," the servant said, leading her away. His tone was not one of kindness, and Thomas was sure his master's emotions would mirror that of the servant's.

He stood there silently in the dark. Feelings of guilt and worry filled his mind.

A few minutes later, Mr. Hiott enter the foyer in his nightclothes. "Captain!" he called out.

"Yes, sir?"

Mr. Hiott pointed a stiff finger in Thomas's direction. "You've put my only daughter in jeopardy tonight. I thought you were a man of sense, but it appears I've been mistaken."

"Sir, we were on a walk when. . ."

"I don't care what you were doing," Mr. Hiott interrupted. "You shouldn't have taken her anywhere near the harbor."

Thomas couldn't argue with him. Mr. Hiott was right. He should have never taken her there. It was a mistake he hoped he could apologize for. But he wouldn't get the chance. Mr. Hiott's vengeance would be swift.

"You will not come back here, Captain. I'm sure I can find a better suitor for my daughter. Perhaps one who cares about her safety. Good evening to you."

Mr. Hiott turned and walked away. Having nothing left to do or say, Thomas opened the door and walked outside. Standing on the porch with his head hung low, he felt defeated, embarrassed, and angry. He didn't expect to encounter these range of emotions. They differed greatly with the ones he had felt earlier in the evening.

Chapter 16

Thomas arrived at his office early. Getting any sleep last night was impossible. He sat down and brought out his notes on the courier murder. He hoped something jumped out at him as he scanned the papers, something that he may have overlooked. Although he felt Rhett LaCroix was his suspect, he had no proof. He knew he should have been surveilling the man yesterday, but his infatuation with Ellen clouded his judgement. He heard someone coming down the hallway and looked up from his desk. Colonel Marlow swept into his office and slammed the door. He rose to attention and saluted.

"Sit down!" the colonel yelled.

Thomas did as the colonel ordered and returned to his chair. An uneasy feeling quickly took hold of him.

The colonel remained standing. "You have done a great deal to embarrass this department, Captain. Have you any idea what I'm referring to?"

Thomas didn't know what to say, but he figured playing dumb may be his best approach. "No, sir."

"You confronted a respected employee at the Bank of Charleston and accused him of being a murderer. Does that sound familiar?"

"I didn't imply he was a murderer, sir."

"Then why did you visit him?" the colonel asked. "Are you looking for a loan of some type?"

Thomas needed to choose his words carefully. He had never seen the colonel this upset before. "I was just following the evidence, sir. There were some similarities between Mr. LaCroix and the spy."

The colonel slammed his fist on Thomas's desk. The sound echoed through the small office. "Be careful with that word! We have nothing to prove the murderer of that courier is a spy!"

Thomas nodded. "I'm sorry, sir. You're right."

The apology seemed to calm the colonel down momentarily. He took a breath a stepped back from the desk. "You are hereby barred from investigating this case further. Bring me all information and any evidence you have on the matter. It needs to be in my office in less than one hour. I will be taking charge of this assignment personally."

"Yes, sir," Thomas replied calmly. There was nothing else to say.

"And one other matter before I leave. I have learned through certain channels that you played a part in the injury of Mr. Hiott's daughter. Make sure you do as you've been told and stay away from her. Any more incidents like these, and I promise your reassignment to a less desirable post. Do I make myself clear, Captain?"

Thomas remained professional and level headed. Although he was angry about this incursion into his personal life, he knew better than to question his superior. It surely would make matters worse. "Perfectly clear, sir."

The colonel left the office as quickly as he entered, closing the door behind him. Thomas sat there in silence. This was it, he thought. He was done chasing the spy. He closed the file on his desk and put the pipe and tobacco into a burlap pouch. Feeling empty and irritated, he buckled on his sword belt and left the office. He handed the items to the first person he saw, Lieutenant

Rhodes. "Take this to the colonel, Rhodes. Make sure it's there in less than an hour."

Thomas walked outside and turned south. He was heading for a drink—a strong one. Recent events had made him weary to say the least. He thought a little time at the tavern could liven his spirits.

He made it two blocks before seeing Inspector James walking in his direction, the ever-present straw hat sitting high upon his head. Thomas hadn't spoken with him since they were at the tobacco shop in the market.

"I was on my way to see you, Thomas," John said, the two shaking hands. "It's about a curious incident involving an officer from Alabama. Happened last night."

Thomas shrugged uninterestingly. He didn't care much about work today, but he figured a story and some company would be nice. "I was going to get a drink. You want to come along?"

Thomas saw John look down at the ground. He knew the inspector was tight with the small amount of money he earned on his job. "I'll buy," Thomas offered.

John smiled and clapped his hands. "Sounds good then. Shall we?"

The two men entered a tavern nearby. The place was small and plain. It wasn't one of the establishments frequented by most officers. They tended to drink at *The Palmetto,* a nicer place further down the peninsula. The two men sat at the bar, both ordering a whiskey.

"Before you tell me anything, I'm letting you know I'm off the courier murder," Thomas advised.

John took a sip and raised his eyebrows. "Made someone mad, did you?" he mused.

Thomas nodded. "Something like that."

"But you're still our liaison, correct?"

"Marlow didn't say anything about that. I guess I am."

"Good," John answered. "In that case, let me tell you about the officer our constable found in the alley."

Thomas wondered why he didn't know about this. "If he was murdered, why weren't we notified?"

John laughed. "There was no murder, my young friend. He was very much alive when he was found—a little drunk though."

Thomas took a sip before answering coolly, "Go on."

"An infantry major was found naked in an alley a block from *The Palmetto.* He told the constable who found him that he was hit over the head by someone, knocking him out. His uniform and pistol were gone when he awoke."

"Why would someone steal his uniform?" Thomas asked curiously. "I can understand the pistol, but the uniform makes no sense."

"I don't know either," John replied, looking into his cup.

Thomas usually had to prod John for additional information. He felt this was one of those times. "What else? I'm sure you have more to tell me."

"Well, he then told the constable he remembered leaving the tavern with a man who had a French accent. He wasn't sure if this was the same one who hit him though."

"Did he remember the man's name?"

John shook his head. "No, he didn't. He wouldn't tell our constable anymore. He begged not to have this matter reported to your people. I guess he knew he would get into trouble."

"He would too," Thomas assured. "That type of conduct wouldn't be tolerated."

"Curious case, though," John said. "The pistol I see, but to strip the man naked and take the uniform—well, that's a new one for me."

Thomas thought for a moment. It wasn't the middle of winter. The homeless in the city were trying to beat the heat, not find more clothes to wear. And the French accent. Again, there was a similarity to Rhett LaCroix.

"Thomas," John said, pulling him out of his apparent trance. "What do you think about all this?"

"I think it's strange," he answered. "You were right to bring this to my attention."

John downed his whiskey and returned the cup to the bar. "If you need anything, I'll be at the station. They're on me about the murder at the Jones house. Any information you find about that one will be more than appreciated."

"Thank you, John. I'll let you know."

John left Thomas sitting there. The tavern keeper walked over with the whiskey bottle in his hand. "Want another, Captain?"

"No, thank you. I have a busy day ahead of me."

Chapter 17

Rhett pulled the floorboard up as quietly as possible. He didn't want to give Mr. Brenton any reason for suspicion. He found the space in the void was just large enough to fit the items. He placed the uniform, boots, and revolver in the hole before putting the floorboard back in place. Knowing the hammering of a nail would be too loud, he pushed his bed over the space to keep it secure. Feeling satisfied, he sat down at his table. He stared at the floor for a moment hoping he had chosen a good spot for the uniform's concealment. It was important to his mission. The uniform would allow him entry into Fort Wagner on the night of the Union assault. Once inside, he would attempt to blow up the powder magazine. The explosion would surely create a hole in the fort's walls, thus allowing his comrades an easy way inside. He felt this was a good plan. He just hoped there were no snags along the way.

After dressing into his suit, he descended the stairs into the tailor shop—Mr. Brenton was not there. Rhett was now displeased that he went to such lengths to be quiet. He contemplated returning to his room with a hammer and nails but decided against it. The current hiding place would be secretive enough.

He found the normal Charleston Sunday scene outside. People were dressed in their finest heading for church. Rhett himself had no need for religion, knowing his enjoyment of murdering made him evil. But he did have a need to attend service today.

As he made his way to St. Michael's Episcopal, he hoped his complaint to the colonel about Captain Altman would be sufficient to ensure his safety. It was apparent that the captain believed him to be the guilty man in both murders. He would have never received a visit from him at the bank had this not been the case.

Rhett was greeted by the usher as he entered the foyer of the church. He told the man he was an acquaintance of the Hiotts and was pointed to a pew where his employer and daughter were seated.

Mr. Hiott stood upon seeing him. "Hello, Rhett. I'm glad you could come today. The two men shook hands.

"I know you invited me months ago, sir. I'm sorry I haven't responded to the invitation until now."

"No worries, have a seat," he answered, motioning to an empty space beside his daughter. "I'm sure Ellen would enjoy your company. She had an unfortunate incident a few nights ago."

Rhett sat down beside Ellen. He saw that her right arm was in a sling. "If you don't mind me asking, what happened to your arm?"

Ellen smiled at him. "I was a little close to the Yankee cannons. The sling is more precautionary than functional. The injury only required stiches."

"I'm glad you weren't hurt worse, ma'am," Rhett said. He was lying, of course.

The three held no further conversation as the service began. Rhett heard the minister giving a fiery sermon about something, but he wasn't listening close enough to understand its contents. His main purpose of his attendance was to get closer to the Hiott family. In truth, he had a plan to leave Charleston a rich man. This would require getting close to Ellen, which he knew would not be difficult to do. In appearance, he was an eligible, handsome bachelor who retained a good position at the bank. He hoped, given this résumé, Mr. Hiott would allow his daughter to court him. This would be necessary to achieve his goal—a goal not sanctioned by the Union army.

When the service ended, the three walked outside. Mr. Hiott stayed on the steps of the church conversing with other members of the congregation while Rhett walked Ellen over to their buggy. The driver opened the door allowing Ellen to step in while Rhett assisted her up the steps.

"May I call on you this evening?" he asked her.

Ellen put her head down. She wasn't smiling as he expected. "I will have to ask my Father. People calling on me has caused some issues of late."

"Don't concern yourself with it then," he replied. I will ask him myself. Hopefully, you will see me if he allows it."

"Very well," Ellen replied without looking up.

Rhett bowed and tipped his hat to her before moving toward Mr. Hiott. The old banker was walking to the buggy.

"Mr. Hiott, sir."

"Yes, Rhett."

"I was wondering if I may call on your daughter this evening."

"I would allow that. To be honest, it would be nice to have someone else besides that silly captain stopping by."

Rhett assumed he was speaking of Altman. "You mean Altman, sir?"

"Yes. Unfortunately for him, he put my daughter in danger. I trust you will not do the same."

"I give you my word, sir."

The two shook hands and Rhett tipped his hat. He stood there for a moment watching the buggy rattle away. Now that the first part of his plan was put into motion, he began to think about his next move.

Chapter 18

Thomas was disobeying the colonel by following Rhett LaCroix, but he didn't care. John's information concerning the theft of the major's uniform was just the thing he needed to assure himself that he was right— LaCroix was his man. Since that was the case, he had tailed him for two days. Saturday was uneventful. The suspect didn't come out of his room above the tailor shop. Today was different though. Thomas kept his distance from the church. He tried to blend in with the people and soldiers on the street, staying as inconspicuous as possible. Standing near the corner of a building looking under the brim of his hat, he saw Ellen walk out the church with LaCroix. His blood boiled at the sight. Not only was the man who he knew to be a Union spy walking around free, the woman he had fallen in love with was now at his side. He tried to calm himself. Getting mad at the situation would do nothing to help him.

After a few minutes, the Hiott's driver snapped the horse's reigns and the buggy drove away from the church. Thomas watched as LaCroix stood there in the street with a large grin on his face. He wondered what the villain was thinking about. Killing, perhaps?

LaCroix began walking south. Thomas followed far behind trying not to draw any attention, but the pedestrians on the street were getting in his way. He pushed a large, slow-moving gentleman aside at one point, the man turning to look at him angrily. "Sorry, sir,"

Thomas replied, tipping his hat. The man nodded in return and he continued his pursuit. He drew closer to LaCroix now, using the man's top hat as a target. Then he was gone. The hat made a right turn and disappeared into a side street. *Could he have seen me?* he wondered. Thomas continued walking, passing the street where LaCroix turned. He made it a short way before stopping to lean against one of the large oak trees that lined the street. Nowhere to go now, he decided to wait.

About twenty minutes later, LaCroix reappeared. He was exiting the street where he had turned into earlier. Carrying a box under his left arm, he tipped his hat to two ladies as he walked in Thomas's direction. Getting behind the tree now, Thomas hoped he wouldn't be spotted. Although a tense moment, LaCroix made his way past him casually, giving no sign of alarm. He then continued his surveillance, following the target to the tailor's shop. Thomas wished he could gain access to his room. Finding something incriminating there would be helpful. He knew all he needed was a shred of evidence-just a little something tying LaCroix to the murders.

Knowing too much time posted outside the shop would draw negative attention, Thomas decided to leave. But he had another matter to attend to anyway: Ellen. The sight of LaCroix being with her disturbed him. He had met a woman who he cared deeply for and had already lost her. Now, this dangerous man was trying to enter her life, and for what purpose, he didn't know.

Turning around, he started toward the Hiott house. He had to talk to her, but he didn't know how. There was no way he would be allowed inside. But this was too important; Ellen had to be warned, no matter the consequences.

His achy knee, coupled with the unusually busy streets, slowed him down a bit getting there. But that gave him time to formulate a plan. He decided to wait outside the home, hoping she would come outside for some fresh air. She had told Thomas how much she detested staying inside all day during one of their conversations. When she did exit, he would make his move. Concealed in an alley across the street, he stared at the house.

It wasn't long before the elements began to cause him some discomfort. The oppressive mid-day heat caused him to sweat profusely. The wagons and buggies travelling the street made his situation worse as well. The wheels stirred up clouds of dust, which choked his already dry throat.

An hour more passed before he decided to take a new approach. If Ellen was inside, he would try and signal her. He had not seen what room belonged to her when he had been given his short tour. He assumed she would stay on the second floor of the mansion, since the dining room and sitting rooms were on the bottom level. He crossed the street focusing on the garden behind the house, which was enclosed by a tall picket fence. Luckily, he found the gate leading from the garden to the street to be unlocked. Opening it, he entered. Thomas started down the stone walkway leading to the back door. Closer now, he looked up, hoping he could catch a glimpse of Ellen looking out of a window. Almost to the steps, he heard the sound of a buggy coming to a stop on the street. Thomas walked over the fence and looked through a small hole in one of the slats. What he saw was disheartening—it was General Ripley. He had to get out. If he were found in the garden uninvited while the general was visiting, his circumstances would surely worsen.

Thomas turned and ran for the gate. His boots were making a clatter as they met the stone walkway. Just before putting his hand on the latch, he heard a voice call his name. He turned to see Ellen running toward him. She didn't slow until she made it into his arms. They embraced—then kissed. Thomas didn't want to let go. But he had to, he couldn't get caught here.

She looked up at him. "What are you doing? You know what Father said."

Thomas grabbed her face gently with both his hands. "I've come to tell you that you are in great danger."

"From whom?" she asked.

"Rhett LaCroix. I have reason to believe the man is a Yankee spy."

Ellen looked curiously at him. "A spy? He's from New Orleans, not the north."

"You just have to believe me," he replied. "I am close to proving it, I promise."

"How will you prove it?" she asked.

"I don't know yet. But you must be cautious of him. Your father needs to as well."

Ellen shook her head. "Father has told me that Rhett is a good man. He will never believe what you are saying."

"I know that," Thomas said, kissing her on her forehead. "But do you?"

Ellen didn't answer. She pulled his face close to her. The two kissed again.

She pushed him a back a few inches, still looking in his eyes. "I do. I promise I do."

"Good," Thomas said, running his hand softly on her injured arm. "The sling is gone. Are you in any pain?"

"Miss Ellen!" a voice called from the house. Thomas could tell it was the doorman he had encountered before.

"Go, quickly," she whispered, not answering the question about her arm.

Thomas didn't have the chance to tell her goodbye. He pushed the gate open and made his way into the street.

He thought about what to do next. It was obvious Mr. Hiott felt Rhett LaCroix was a standup gentleman, although this wasn't the truth. He would have to prove he was right to save many lives and perhaps the city. But this meant taking risks, having courage. The last time he had to show courage, however, was at the Battle Sharpsburg. It didn't go well. He hoped this time would be different.

Chapter 19

Lieutenant Chase accompanied Thomas to the office this morning. The young man was released from sick call yesterday. Thomas was extremely pleased. He would have someone he could trust now. Someone on whom he could depend.

His plan this morning was to talk the colonel into allowing him back on the murder investigation. Thomas would give Marlow a sincere apology and promise to focus on other suspects. This would be a lie though. He knew who he would focus on. He had already told Chase about his findings before they made it to the provost marshal building.

"What would be sufficient evidence to prove this man is a spy, sir?" Chase asked Thomas, as they crossed the busy intersection of Calhoun and Meeting Streets.

"We need something other than theories, Lieutenant. If we were to find that Major's uniform in LaCroix's possession, that would prove everything."

"How would we do that sir?"

"Without kicking in the door and searching his room, I don't know," Thomas explained. "But first, I have to get back in the colonel's good graces."

Once in the building, they parted ways. When Thomas made it to his office and opened the door he saw a folded letter sitting on the desk. It was out of the ordinary to receive correspondence without it being hand delivered. That being the case, he had an immediate concern about its contents. He hung his hat on a hook by the door and sat down at his desk. Opening the letter, he began to read:

Captain T. Altman,

You are to report to Richmond, Virginia, to serve in the office of the provost marshal there. Proceed by rail to Florence, SC, where you will switch trains bound for the aforementioned location. Major Vincent will be your new commanding officer.

J. Marlow, Colonel

Thomas put the letter on the desk and stared at it. He assumed Mr. Hiott must not have been content with just embarrassing him, he wanted him away from Ellen for good. This was a man, after all, who had thrown an expensive dinner party for the highest-ranking officers. He had money and power; Thomas had neither of those. He would have to leave the woman and the city he loved. There would be no chance of capturing LaCroix now. It was over.

Lieutenant Chase walked into the office with an uncomfortable expression on his face. "Are you alright, Captain?"

"Someone told you already?" Thomas asked, already knowing the answer.

"As soon as I walked away from you, sir."

Thomas stood up and walked to the window. He ran his right hand through his hair as he stared outside. "I have been outmatched, Chase. I can't help but think Mr. LaCroix has something to do with this." Thomas turned around and looked wearily at the lieutenant. "Not only has he destroyed me, he'll help the Yankees destroy the city."

Chase stiffened at the comment. "I can prove that he is a spy, sir."

Thomas cut him off, waving his hand. "You should do what you are ordered to do. There's no need for you to get yourself into trouble."

Chase dropped his head. "Very well, sir."

"Good," Thomas replied. "I wish you the best in your work here. You've been an excellent aide and a brave gentleman."

"Thank you, sir," Chase said, attempting a smile. "I will get Corporal Jackson to gather your belongings."

Chase saluted before leaving the office. Thomas returned the salute and went back to looking out the window. He could see it now. The United States Army triumphantly parading down the street, its soldiers mocking the citizens of Charleston who watched them nervously. It was a thought that was too much to bear. Had he arrested LaCroix, maybe this wouldn't happen. But he hadn't. Forces would now be put into motion that he couldn't stop.

Corporal Jackson entered the office and gave a salute. Thomas didn't have the desire to salute back. Instead, he pointed to the chair in front of his desk. "Have a seat, Corporal."

"Yes, sir.

The corporal was a young man, barely twenty, with fiery red hair. Thomas thought what a shame it would be if this youthful soldier lost his life keeping the Yankees out of the city. Nothing he could do now, though. He scribbled a short note asking the sergeant at the barracks to pack his belongings. He then ordered Corporal

Jackson to bring the items and meet him here at noon. The corporal took the note and quickly made his way out of the office. After collecting the few small items that were left in his desk, he left the building and headed for St. Phillip Street—police headquarters. If no one in the military would believe him, maybe the civilian authorities would. He hoped John was there. He could only share this information with him. But after that meeting was concluded, Thomas had one more stop to make. He had to see her one last time.

Chapter 20

He sat at the colonel's desk preparing to work. But he wasn't trying his best to make sure the numbers were right. Rhett knew his mission here was almost over, and he no longer cared about pleasing the colonel. Soon, he hoped to be watching the city's capture from the deck of a Union warship. He would be puffing on his pipe while doing so, the same pipe he had just removed from the colonel's desk drawer. He was happy to be reacquainted with it. It was a treat he didn't expect. He had no clue that his complaint made the colonel remove Altman from the courier's investigation. He slipped the pipe in his coat pocket and began to adjust the ledger. As he dipped his pen in the inkwell, he heard some movement in the hallway. *There shouldn't be anyone here,* he thought. He heard a key turn in the lock before the door opened. It was the colonel.

"You decided to come today?" the colonel asked, closing the door behind him. His voice was laden with sarcasm.

Rhett hadn't shown up yesterday. He knew he probably should have, but he was losing his desire to help the rebel make money. "I'm sorry I didn't come, sir. Some issues at the bank required my attention after hours."

The colonel took off his gloves and hat. He dropped them on the table angrily. "Do you think the gold I pay you comes easily to me?"

"No, sir," Rhett casually answered.

The colonel pointed at the ledger. "You see how slim of a profit I make from my business ventures. This profit becomes much smaller if my records aren't kept properly. I've already had to chastise you once concerning this same matter, don't you recall?"

Rhett knew he should just answer like the good employee. Disagreeing with the colonel would do no good. But today, he felt differently. In front of him stood a high-ranking, and very corrupt, rebel officer. And since his time here was ending, he saw no reason to continue his relationship with the colonel. It was time to end this. "I do recall, sir," Rhett replied, slowly standing up. "But now, I would like to ask you some questions."

The colonel shot him an angry look. "Excuse me?"

Rhett walked closer to him, hands behind his back, and a devious grin on his face. "Does anyone know I work for you, sir?"

"No, why do you ask?"

"Just curious, sir. I would hate for anyone to learn I keep the books for a corrupt officer who sells stolen cotton to the enemy."

The colonel pointed a finger at Rhett's face. He was red with anger. "You watch yourself, boy. You forget who you're talking to."

Rhett began to slowly circle the colonel. "I know who I am talking to, Colonel. I'm talking to a man who is the worst kind of rebel, a dirty one."

The colonel reached for his gun holster and pulled up the flap. Rhett lunged forward and grabbed his hand. A frightened look appeared on Marlow's face, but he didn't attempt to pull away.

"Easy Colonel, no need for that," Rhett said, holding the colonel's hand firmly, being sure not to release the grip. "I will be the only one doing the killing here tonight."

The colonel tried to pull away from Rhett while using his left hand to throw a punch. Rhett ducked as the fist past inches above his head. He then pulled his Bowie knife from the sheath tucked into the back of his trousers. Before the colonel could recover from his missed blow, Rhett plunged the knife deep into his stomach. He watched as Marlow's mouth opened to speak, but nothing came out. Rhett pulled his knife back, letting the colonel fall to the floor. The colonel's eyes began to turn gray; he was dead.

Rhett took the handkerchief from his pocket and wiped the blood from the knife. He was glad he killed him. He had not planned on doing this, but what was done was done. There had been too many times that John Marlow had talked down to him. There would be no more. He grabbed the body by the feet and pulled it across the room away from the door. Someone would surely open the office to find Marlow dead in a few hours, but he would be long gone by that time. He took his coat off the back of the desk chair and put it on. He then picked up the ledger and tucked it underneath his arm. His Union army bosses would be glad to learn that some of their own officers were making money on these illegal shipments. He envisioned a pat on the back from Abe Lincoln himself when this information was brought to light. Maybe even a promotion.

He checked to make sure the door was locked behind him when he left the office. Rhett walked to the staircase, descended to the bottom floor, and entered the alley. He felt the excitement of victory. The colonel was dead, he had avoided any suspicion concerning the murders, and the Union army would take Morris Island in two days. Everything was going to plan. But he needed to finish his business with Mr. Hiott for his time here to be completely fulfilled. He didn't plan on leaving Charleston with just his pipe.

Chapter 21

Thomas shifted on an uncomfortable wooden bench at the train station. He was flanked on each side by civilian passengers who, like he, waited for the next outbound train. Many of the city's residents were choosing to evacuate now. The food shortages were taking its toll on their health and spirits. Although not made to leave, the choice to stay was a risky one. But unlike them, Thomas wanted to stay. He missed the place already. After leaving the barracks, he had tried to see Ellen. Unfortunately, the attempt ended as he thought it would. The house servant ordered him away before slamming the door in his face. To add to his frustration, John wasn't at the police station when he called on him. He knew there was no way he could stay any longer. The colonel would surely arrest him for disobeying orders if he didn't leave immediately.

The locomotive's horn blew twice announcing its approach before stopping. Thomas moved onto the platform. He stood up and motioned for Corporal Jackson to bring his luggage. As he walked to the passenger car, Jackson following close behind, he thought he heard someone calling his name. He stopped, looked around, saw nothing. Then he heard it again. Clearer this time.

"Captain Altman!" the voice yelled.

Thomas stepped back from the train and waited for the crowd of passengers to thin out. It was then he saw Lieutenant Chase. The officer was calling his name while running down the platform.

"Chase, over here!" Thomas shouted.

When Thomas finally caught Chase's attention, he could see that the lieutenant appeared overly excited. They met each other just in front of the ticket booth.

Chase had to catch his breath before speaking. "You have to come back, sir. The colonel has been murdered."

Thomas was shocked; he didn't know what to think. Immediately, LaCroix came to mind. Marlow had taken over the investigation of the courier murder. He thought LaCroix may have taken a new approach at murdering. He would now be eliminating the men who were trying to capture him.

"What do we know?" Thomas asked.

"Nothing, sir," Chase answered. "He was found dead in his office this morning. The last time anyone saw him was yesterday afternoon."

"How was he killed?"

"Stabbed in the stomach, sir," Chase replied, with a strange look on his face.

Thomas noticed the expression. "What are you thinking?"

"Well, sir, it seems like the courier and the colonel were both killed the same way. The stab wound was in the same location. It might just be a coincidence, but I get a strange feeling that it might be the same killer."

Thomas didn't respond to the theory. Instead, he was more curious as to why Chase was even here. "Did someone send you to get me?"

"General Ripley, sir. But I must tell you that he is slightly suspicious of you at the moment."

Being a professional, Thomas could see why. He had just been relieved of his duties and ordered away. He was also sure the general heard of the incident with Ellen. "I don't blame him, Lieutenant," he said, "but you know I had nothing to do with it, don't you?

Chase gave him a wide-eyed look. "Of course, sir."

Thomas moved on to the reason for the lieutenant coming. "I'm assuming you weren't sent here just to tell me that. And it doesn't appear you want to arrest me either."

"You are right, sir. I'm here to tell you that the general wants you to come back. That's all I'm allowed to say."

Thomas was nervous at what he was going back to, but at least he was going back. "Well then, let's get to it, Lieutenant." He then turned to Corporal Jackson. "Take the luggage back to the barracks. I'll unpack later."

The corporal saluted and walked away, the suitcases in tow.

Thomas and Chase walked to an awaiting wagon back at the street. Once both men were inside, the private at the reigns was ordered to proceed back to the provost marshal's building.

"Where am I to meet the general?" Thomas asked Chase, having to speak louder than usual to be heard above the clattering wheels.

"The colonel's office, sir. He wants you to see it for yourself."

Thomas didn't have any more questions. He remained quiet the rest of the ride thinking about this strange turn of events. The colonel was murdered, he was staying in the city, and he may be able to see Ellen. But then he thought about Rhett LaCroix. He knew he was right about the man, and he knew he had to be stopped.

They came to a stop in front of the building. Once inside, Thomas found the place much quieter than usual. There were no questions or smiles from any of the men, only salutes and nods. It was evident the murder had caused a great deal of shock within the department.

Up the stairs, Thomas encountered a private guarding the colonel's door. He could hear people talking inside as he made his way closer.

"No entry, sir," the private standing guard at the door advised.

"That's alright, let him in," Thomas heard General Ripley say from inside the office.

The private moved out of the way allowing Thomas and Chase to pass. Both men snapped to attention and saluted the general. There were two other men with the general, a major and a lieutenant colonel. Thomas assumed both men were Ripley's aides.

The general returned the salute. "At ease, gentlemen. Everyone, please excuse the captain and me for a moment."

The remaining people in the room shuffled out, closing the door behind them. Ripley stood in the middle of the office, calmly smoking a cigar. Thomas realized the smoking was more to mask the disturbing smell of the corpse than for mere pleasure. The undeniable smell of death lingered heavily within the walls of the office.

"Go have a look," the general ordered, pointing across the room.

Thomas found the colonel's body behind the desk. He could tell the murder wasn't freshly committed, as the body had started to show signs of rigor mortis. Thomas knelt down. He looked at the body closer, seeing the colonel was indeed killed by a single stab wound to the stomach. Interestingly, the colonel's gun was still in its holster. He thought that was strange. The colonel must have known and trusted the assailant, since he didn't anticipate an attack. Had he sensed danger, the gun would have surely been drawn to counter the threat.

"What do you think, Captain?" Ripley asked, walking up behind Thomas.

"Well sir, I'm most intrigued by the colonel's revolver still being in the holster. I assume he was trusting of the killer. Probably let him in the office not thinking this would happen," Thomas said before pausing to rub his knee. "Whoever it was also had access to building. Anyone coming inside after hours would be checked by the guards at the front door. Only the colonel uses the back entrance off the alley. He had the only key, if I remember correctly."

The general folded his arms and gave Thomas a serious look. "Given everything you've just told me, wouldn't the best suspect be someone who was assigned to this department?"

"It would seem so, sir," Thomas agreed.

"So," Ripley began, "you can see why I initially thought you might have had something to do with this."

Thomas agreed with the general. He knew if it were him, he would have thought the same thing. But he didn't get the chance to respond. As he opened his mouth, the general waved his hand.

"No need to answer, Altman. I know you would agree me with me on that. I'm confident that a man who just murdered his superior officer would be much harder to find than you were this morning. Besides, Lieutenant Chase informed me you were at the barracks all night."

"Thank you, sir," Thomas replied. He was relieved he didn't have to profess his innocence like he thought he may have to.

"Now, get an assistant and begin working on this. And I want to be kept apprised of what's going on, do you understand?"

"Yes, sir, I do."

"Good, I'll be back and forth between my headquarters and Morris Island. The Yankee infantry is landing there as we speak. I believe they will try to attack Wagner again very soon."

"Yes, sir," Thomas said, saluting the general.

"One more thing," Ripley said, turning around at the door. "Hiott told me about the business with his daughter."

Thomas was embarrassed. Again, there was nothing to say.

"I know it must be hard for you to stay away," the general began, "but you need to focus on this assignment. Put all your energy into finding out what happened here."

The general then left the room, not waiting on a reply.

Thomas appreciated the general's words and knew he was right. Today was a chance to start anew, to bring this man, this spy, this murderer, to justice. He had to do his best work now. Everything else could wait.

He went back over to the colonel's body, examining it once more. Thomas wondered if he should have told the general he did have a suspect, but without evidence, it was only speculation. Going after LaCroix had already backfired once. He knew he had to play the game better this time, be smarter than his opponent. He looked away from the body and focused on the colonel's desk. A bottom drawer was slightly ajar. He thought that was odd. Every other drawer was closed except for this one. Nothing else in the office looked to be disturbed. He fully opened the drawer and looked inside. There was the pouch of tobacco he had given as evidence to the colonel. The strange thing was not what he found in the drawer; but what was missing: the pipe. His heart beat faster, knowing this was a sign that he was right. He closed the drawer and left the office. A mortician and two of his assistants stood in the hallway, ready to take the body. Behind them stood Chase and the private who had been ordered to guard the door.

"All yours," Thomas said, moving past the morticians.

Thomas pulled Chase aside. "We're back on the hunt, Lieutenant. I hope you're ready."

Chapter 22

There wasn't much for Rhett to do today, but that was good. It gave him time to prepare for the grand finale—the end of his mission. He was nothing short of excited now; giddy, even. He would leave here a hero, and if things went according to plan, a rich hero.

He walked out of his office into the bank lobby. Several people were at the teller windows making deposits and withdrawals- the normal business of the day. Then he heard it. It was the sound of distant cannon fire. Rhett walked outside and looked toward the south end of town. A man in a brown suit with a matching top hat stopped beside him.

"The cannon fire seems to be increasing. Do you think the Yankees will try and enter the harbor again?" the man asked.

Rhett smiled. "I do not believe so, sir. Fort Sumter has been impregnable so far. I believe the Yankees will try and take Morris Island to establish a base from which to assault Sumter."

The man turned and looked at him. Rhett could see he was impressed by what he had just heard.

"Seems like you know a lot about military matters, sir. Were you in the army?"

"No, sir, I was not," Rhett answered. "But I put myself in the position of the enemy. If it were me, that's the way I would try to take the city."

The man grabbed his lapels and bowed out his chest. "Ha! They may try, sir, but I can assure you the city will not fall. One southern soldier is worth at least three Yankees. Good day to you." With that, the man continued down the street.

Rhett was used to hearing this from the rebels. They believed the Union army could never defeat the South, but he knew their arrogance would not last for long; he knew the real reason for the cannon fire. The Union Navy was bombarding Fort Wagner to smash its defenses. Once its walls were weakened, the infantry would assault the bastion under the cover of darkness. With his help, they would surely be victorious. He pulled his silver pocket watch and checked the time—five o'clock. It was time to leave.

The walk to his room was easier than normal. The cannon fire had coerced many of the usual pedestrians to remain indoors. Entering Mr. Brenton's shop, Rhett saw his landlord sitting on a crate behind the counter, head in his hands. It was clear he was concerned about something. Rhett put his briefcase on the counter. "What's wrong, Mr. Brenton?" he asked. "You look unwell, sir."

Mr. Brenton stood up and removed his spectacles. After wiping them off with a handkerchief, he put them back on and shook his head. "There's been some sort of problem upstairs, Rhett."

"Upstairs? My room, you mean?"

"Apparently so. Three men showed up here this morning. They demanded I give them the key to your room. Two were with the provost marshal and one was a city constable."

Rhett felt a knot in his throat, but he tried to hide any emotion. He didn't want to seem suspicious. "I don't know what they could want. I'm just a lowly bank employee, struggling like everyone else."

Mr. Brenton looked down, shaking his head. "I don't need any trouble with the authorities. I had no choice but to do as they requested."

Rhett managed an easing smile. "I'm sure this is some misunderstanding," he said in a calm voice. "There's nothing in my room anyone could want."

"I hope not," Mr. Brenton replied. "I was told by Mr. Hiott that you would be a good lodger."

"Have I ever given you a reason to assume otherwise?" Rhett retorted.

Mr. Brenton cocked his head to the side in a gesture of agreeance. "No, you haven't."

"Then I'll be on my way. I hope those men don't waste any more of our time."

"I do as well, Rhett. I do as well."

"Good evening, Mr. Brenton."

"Good evening."

Rhett started to perspire as he walked up the stairs. He was nervous to see what was missing from his room—if anything. *Surely, they would have come for me if they had found it,* he thought. He put his key in the door and turned the lock. He threw it open to find everything in its place, save one drawer that was slightly ajar. He ran over to the bed and pushed it a few feet from its location. The floorboard hadn't been disturbed, but he reached down and pulled it up anyway. The major's uniform, revolver, and the colonel's ledger were still in its hiding place. He let out a deep breath trying to calm himself. If it would have been found, his mission was compromised, and he was a dead man. He returned the floorboard and moved the bed back on top of it. Pulling up a chair, he began to smoke his pipe. The tobacco helped him feel better, helped clear his head. He sat there wondering why they searched his room. Altman was no longer investigating him, and the colonel was dead. He thought that was the end of it. But as he took a long pull from the pipe, it occurred to him, *they think I killed him*. He began to ask himself questions: *Did the colonel lie to me about someone knowing I was an employee? Did I leave something in the office that could identify me?* He wasn't sure of anything, and it bothered him.

He finished his smoke. Knowing he could achieve nothing by endless worrying, he began to get ready for dinner. He changed into a clean suit and donned a fresh neck tie. Both were black. His knife was tucked into the back of his trousers in its usual position. Checking himself in the small mirror on the desk, he noticed his whiskers weren't as crisp on the ends as he preferred. He must have pulled on them while he was smoking his pipe, a habit he had tried, unsuccessfully, to break. Fixing his mustache, he was ready now to leave.

Descending the stairs into the tailor shop, he found Mr. Brenton still there. The tailor was diligently sewing a pair of trousers on his work table. He turned to Rhett when he entered the shop. "They didn't touch anything, Mr. Brenton. Must have been a misunderstanding."

"I'm sure it was, Rhett. I thought it strange they would think you were involved in something illegal."

"Rest assured, sir, I'm doing nothing but trying to make a living," Rhett said, moving closer to the tailor. "But I do have one question."

"What's that?"

"These men, what did they look like?"

Mr. Brenton stopped working and looked up, as if trying to remember their descriptions. "Well, the older man was a city policeman. He wore a faded brown suit and a straw planter's hat. One of the soldiers was a young man, a lieutenant. His face was bruised, looked like he'd been in a scuffle recently. The other officer was a little older. Good looking lad, tall with sharp blue eyes."

That wasn't what Rhett wanted to hear. The last officer was Altman. The same man who he thought had been put on the shelf. It was horrible news. The truth was, Altman wasn't inept like most of the rebel officers he had encountered. He seemed smart and observant. It wasn't the type of man he needed tracking his movements. "Thank you for the information, sir. I'll try to be quiet when coming in later."

Mr. Brenton nodded and returned to sewing. Rhett ventured outside to find a black man dressed in a dark gray suit with a top hat climbing down off the seat of his buggy. "You Mister LaCroix, sir?"

"Yes, who are you?"

The man removed his hat and bowed before speaking. "Mr. Hiott sent me round to pick you up, sir. The boss told me to make sure you wasn't walking to his house tonight."

Rhett smiled, happy to see he was important enough to be offered transportation. "I am who you seek."

The servant opened the door of the buggy and allowed Rhett inside. When the door was closed, and the servant was back at the reigns, Rhett stopped him. "Wait a moment. How will you be signaled to pick me up when I'm ready to leave?"

The servant turned around. "Samuel, the do'man, rings a bell, sir. I'll get up there good and quick after that."

"Thank you, drive on."

Chapter 23

Thomas, Chase, and John left LaCroix's room empty-handed. Thomas was confident LaCroix would leave a clue there proving he was a Union spy, but he found nothing of the sort. He knew he had no legal reason to search the place, but desperate times called for desperate measures. He had crossed the line into illegality, and he knew it. But something had to be done. The death count had risen to three now; the last being the provost marshal himself. John came along at his request, just in case the civilian authorities were alerted of the search. Luckily for Thomas though, John was eager to be there. The inspector hoped he would find something that would help him solve the murder of Mr. Jones's servant—a murder which his superiors were desperately encouraging him to solve.

"I'll deny any knowledge of this if I'm asked," John said to Thomas, as the three men stopped in front of the provost marshal building. "You know we had no right to enter the man's room."

"I understand," Thomas replied. "I just hate that we didn't find anything."

John shrugged. "I do as well. You know how bad I need to solve that murder. Randall Jones has been at headquarters every day asking if we have any leads," John said before tipping his hat. "Have a good evening, gentlemen."

Thomas waited until John was out of earshot to speak to Chase. "He wants him as badly as we do."

"I can see that, sir," Chase agreed. "What do we do next?"

"Go back and get some rest at the barracks. There's nothing more you can do tonight."

"Are you sure, sir?"

"Yes, I'll be fine."

Chase threw up a quick salute before walking off.

Thomas realized he hadn't eaten since the morning. He walked two blocks to a small tavern, one he hadn't been to before. The place had no name, no sign. He saw there were several tables on the outside near the door. He sat down, happy to be off his feet for a moment. The tavern keeper, an older woman wearing a faded blue dress, appeared at the table.

"Nice evening isn't it, Captain?" she asked.

"Yes, ma'am, very nice."

"What can I get you?"

"Coffee if you have any."

"We do. Anything to eat?"

"A couple of biscuits would be wonderful."

The woman nodded. "I'll be right back."

Thomas sat watching a regiment of Georgia troops marching past the tavern. They looked fresh, not beaten down like the men who manned the forts around the harbor. He assumed they would be going to reinforce Fort Wagner.

The column came to an abrupt stop. Thomas heard officers ordering the men to take a break. Appearing out of the mass of gray troops was a weary looking soldier who began to make his way toward Thomas. He was a captain as well, but much younger. He approached the table and saluted. "Captain Estes with the 4th Georgia. May I sit with you, Captain?"

"By all means," Thomas said, shaking the captain's hand and introducing himself.

The two men sat down, and the captain removed his hat. Estes looked tired. His beard was scruffy, needing a trim, and his face was dirty. Thomas assumed he and his men had been on the march for days.

"Where are you men headed?" Thomas asked.

"Some island in the harbor. Can't remember what the colonel said its name was."

The two men were interrupted by the woman returning with Thomas's coffee and food. Captain Estes eyed the cup intently as it was placed on the table. "Is there any more, ma'am?" he asked. "I've been craving a good cup since we left Augusta."

The woman smiled. "Of course, Captain. I'll get you some."

"You men have marched all the way from Augusta?" Thomas inquired.

"Not the whole way," Estes answered. "We were transported by train from there to Columbia. I wasn't told why we couldn't just ride the train all the way here. Maybe the Yankee cavalry was tearing up tracks."

"Well, we're glad you boys could make it," Thomas remarked graciously. "We'll take all the help we can get." Thomas took a sip of his coffee. The hot beverage was just what he needed. Since the blockade had begun, coffee beans had become quite the rarity.

A cannon fired in the distance.

"Where is that fire coming from?" Estes asked.

"The Yankee navy is firing on Wagner," Thomas answered. "This has been going on for the past week. That's probably where you fellas are headed."

Estes snapped his fingers. "That's it, Wagner. That's the name of the place. How important is the fort to the city's defense?"

Before Thomas could answer, the tavern keeper came back with the captain's coffee. Thomas waited for her to walk away before answering. "Pretty important. If it falls, they'll be close enough to fire on Fort Sumter from land."

A look of worry crossed Estes's face. "That's not good. I was hoping we would be put in a quiet sector somewhere."

Thomas shook his head. "It's definitely not going to be quiet if you are out there. You have my word on that."

"Well, they'll eventually take the place then," Estes said. "I've learned that if the Yankees want something bad enough, they're going to get it. They'll use all their men, all their munitions, even spies to win the smallest battle. It makes you wonder how long we can last against an enemy like that."

Those words struck a chord with Thomas. It made him think. If the Union forces were preparing for a major assault on Fort Wagner, maybe that's why LaCroix was here. And if the attack to capture the fort was coming soon, LaCroix's mission would soon be over. Thomas realized that would make him even more dangerous, even more desperate. Thomas heard a horse and buggy coming his direction. The Georgia soldiers who had amassed in the street began to make way, allowing the buggy through. And there he was - Rhett LaCroix. He was dressed in a black suit with a matching top hat, sitting proudly inside, nodding at the soldiers. But the worst part was that it wasn't his buggy—it was Mr. Hiott's. Thomas knew he had to get to the Hiott house; he had to get to Ellen.

"I must be going, Captain. You can eat those biscuits if you are hungry," Thomas said, pointing to the table.

Captain Estes smiled. "Thank you, sir. I'll take care of them for you."

With that, Thomas left a five dollar note on the table and made his way down the street.

Chapter 24

The brisk ride to Mr. Hiott's house was pleasant for Rhett. It gave him time to regain his composure. The search of his room had rattled him, but he was hopeful nothing would come of it.

"Good evenin' sir," the servant greeted Rhett as he entered the house.

"Good evening," he replied. After giving his hat to the doorman, he was shown to the dining room. Waiting for him were Mr. Hiott and Ellen. Both were dressed in their formal dinner wear. Ellen wore a dark blue dress that fit her perfectly. The garment was accented by a shiny silver locket that hung from a chain around her neck. Mr. Hiott wore a dark black suit with coattails, a white vest, and a white necktie.

"Ah, Rhett, come in and have a seat," Mr. Hiott said. The banker stood up and met him halfway to the table to shake his hand.

Rhett then took his seat beside Ellen. She offered no greeting or immediate conversation. He thought that was strange.

A servant brought the dinner to the table. He filled the glasses with wine and asked Mr. Hiott if he could retire for the night. Mr. Hiott nodded at him, thereby granting the request.

"So, Rhett," Mr. Hiott began, "any issues at the bank today?"

"None sir. It was a good day to catch up on some paperwork from earlier in the week."

"Good. Perhaps the Yankees will abandon their attempts to take the city soon. When that happens, we'll be better able to serve the interests of the citizens."

Rhett nodded and looked over at Ellen. Being a spy, he was good at reading people. Something was wrong with her and he wanted to know what. "You look worried, Miss Ellen. Is something the matter?"

A nervous half-smile appeared on her face. "I'm fine, sir. Still shaken up from that incident at the battery."

"I'm sure you were," Rhett answered confidently. "That Altman should have known better than to take you there."

Ellen's nervous smile disappeared. It gave way to a look of anger. "I knew the risk in going, Mr. LaCroix. I could have told him no, but I wanted to be with him. I wanted to go."

Mr. Hiott slammed his hand on the table. "Enough! This is why you are not to see this man again. He is dangerous and careless. In fact, he has been sent away to Virginia. I personally saw to that."

Ellen looked furiously at her father before beginning to cry. She stood up quickly and retired to the sitting room. Mr. Hiott took a sip of his wine and returned the glass to the table.

Rhett could see he was upset about having to scold her. But in this exchange, he saw an opportunity. "I apologize, sir. I shouldn't have brought that up. I meant no harm when I started talking about that man."

"It's alright," Mr. Hiott replied. "You spoke the truth about what happened."

"I would like to speak with Ellen in private to apologize. Could I have a moment to do so?"

Mr. Hiott waved his hand. "You may."

"Thank you. I'll be back in a moment."

Rhett entered the sitting room. Ellen was sitting in a chair crying into a handkerchief. He closed the door behind him. The clicking of the door's mechanism drew her attention.

"What are you doing here?" she asked in an angry tone.

Rhett sat down in a chair across from her. "I've come to explain what's going to happen tonight."

"What are you talking about?"

"First, let me tell you that I'm a dangerous man - very dangerous. While I've been in the city, I've killed several people. And all of this has been done in the name of the U.S. government."

Ellen's eyes widened, and she jumped up from her chair.

Rhett remained calm and seated. "Sit down and be quiet or your father dies."

Ellen looked at him wide-eyed. She did as she was told and returned to her chair. "Who are you?"

"There's no need to go into that. Just do as I say, and no one is harmed."

Rhett reached behind him and pulled the Bowie knife. He walked over to her and held it inches from her face. "Do not try to run or scream. Understand?"

She slowly nodded.

He used the point of the knife to lift her chin. He wanted to see her eyes. "Now, I want you to quietly open the door and go upstairs to your room. I will be right behind you the entire way. If your father calls out for you, tell him everything is fine."

Ellen stood up and walked to the door. Opening it quietly, she and Rhett made their way into the hallway.

Mr. Hiott never called out to her, apparently not hearing the movement in the corridor. Rhett pushed the point of the knife against her back making her ascend the stairs. At the top, Ellen opened the first door she came to and went inside. Rhett closed the door behind them. He ordered her to lay on the bed. She complied. He opened one of her dresser drawers and retrieved three silk waistbands.

"Please don't kill me," Ellen begged in a low voice.

"I won't kill you, just be quiet."

Rhett ordered her to roll over on her stomach. Again, she did as she was told. He then tied her hands behind her back using one of the waistbands. Her feet were tied together next. The last waistband was used to gag her. He didn't need her yelling for help.

He rolled her back over. "Listen to me. If you try and leave this house, or get help of any kind, both you and your father die. I'm taking him with me for a few hours. If everything goes well, you will both be released when I return."

Ellen nodded.

Rhett looked at her once more before leaving, satisfied that she would be going nowhere. And that was good, because he was going to kill her when he came back later.

He made his way back down the stairs. Mr. Hiott was still seated at the table.

"Is she alright?" he asked Rhett.

"She is fine, for now."

Mr. Hiott looked at him curiously. "What do you mean, *for now?*"

Rhett didn't answer the question. "Are there any more servants here, sir?"

"No. Samuel was the only one here tonight."

"Well then, I have nothing to worry about when I tell you that you are coming with me," Rhett explained, pulling out his knife. "You and I are going to the bank tonight. I'm going to take all the gold I want from the vault."

Mr. Hiott stood up looking perplexed. "What in the devil are you talking about? Is this some kind of jest?"

"Oh no, sir, this is no jest," he calmly replied.

"I'm going nowhere with you," Mr. Hiott said defiantly while folding his arms.

"Yes, you are," Rhett replied, scratching his chin lightly with the blade of the knife. "Because if you don't do exactly what I tell you, I will cut your daughter to pieces slowly." He moved the knife through the air in a few short motions. "If you don't believe me, try and call for help. Go ahead, yell as loud as you can."

Mr. Hiott stiffened, but made no reply.

Rhett smiled. "Good. I can see you aren't going to play the part of the hero. Now, go to the front door and ring the bell that signals the horse and buggy. I would like to ride to the bank instead of walking."

Rhett pushed his hostage to the door. Mr. Hiott opened it and rang the doorman's bell three times. In less than a few seconds, the buggy arrived in front. The same driver that brought Rhett to the house climbed down to assist the men up.

"Stay at the reigns, Sammy," Mr. Hiott ordered holding up his hand. "Take us to the bank and do it quickly."

"Yessir." The driver bowed slightly and returned to the seat.

As the buggy drove off, Rhett was excited about his future. Everything was going to plan—or so he thought. Upstairs in the Hiott house, Ellen was working hard to free herself. She was almost out of her restraints.

Chapter 25

It was dark now. He had been hiding in the garden of the Hiott house, ducked low behind a pair of bushes for the past hour. Thomas hoped for two things: to see Ellen and for Rhett LaCroix to leave the house. In a perfect world, the spy would have already been under arrest. But he had to be careful after being given the reprieve from General Ripley. He needed hard evidence to bring LaCroix down.

Outside the garden gate, the servant who brought LaCroix was asleep at the reigns, head down, snoring loudly. Thomas hoped he would be awake soon, driving LaCroix home. This would be his cue. Thomas missed Ellen beyond all logical reason and had to see her. Additionally, he was uncomfortable and hoped for some relief. His knee had started to ache. The crouching he was doing to conceal himself was beginning to take its toll. He thought about leaving, trying again tomorrow. The sound of a bell ringing caught his attention. Thomas looked at the buggy through the slats in the fence. The servant awoke from his slumber, straightened his hat, and snapped the reigns. The buggy lurched forward and stopped in front of the door. Two men climbed inside. He couldn't tell their identities but hoped one of them was LaCroix. If it was though, he had a decision to make. Thomas didn't know if he should follow his suspect or try and see Ellen.

The buggy drove off. He stayed put. He left the concealment of the bushes and walked up the lighted walkway to the house. Just knocking and asking for her wouldn't work; he had to get inside. Thomas made it to the back door and put his hand on the doorknob. He was nervous, not sure what would happen to him if Mr. Hiott was on the other side of the door. He was chancing that he was one of the men who left in the buggy. It was then he heard a yell for help. It was Ellen. He pushed the door open. Again, a scream. He ran to the foyer at the front of the house to see her coming down the stairs. She looked terrified.

"Thomas!" she shouted, leaping off the bottom stair and into his arms.

"What's happened? Are you alright?" he asked.

She held him tightly but didn't speak.

"Are you alright?" he asked again.

"No, he has my father! Please, we have to help him!"

"Calm down," Thomas said. "Who has your father?"

"Rhett LaCroix," she replied, her voice shaky with fear. "He said he was going to kill us both if I didn't do what he said."

"Do you know where they are going?"

"I don't know. He didn't say what he was planning to do."

Thomas wondered for a moment why Mr. Hiott was being kidnapped. But then it came to him. "Who can access the vault at the bank?"

"Only him, no one else."

"They have to be going there," Thomas speculated. "I'll go after him, but you have to stay."

Ellen stepped back and looked at him angrily. "I'm coming with you!"

"It's too dangerous, you can't."

"I'm coming," she demanded. "You'll have to tie me up to keep me here; but as you can see, that won't work." She held up one arm to show Thomas a black waistband tied loosely around one of her wrists.

He could see there would be no stopping her. After all, it was her father who was in danger—he didn't blame her for wanting to go. "Fine, but you must do what I say. I can't have something happen to you."

"I will," she replied.

They ran out into the night.

Chapter 26

As the buggy rattled down the street, Rhett had the point of his knife nestled close to Mr. Hiott's side. He hoped the affluent banker wouldn't try to be a hero tonight—it would only complicate matters.

"How much do you want?" Mr. Hiott asked in a low voice.

"All of it," Rhett replied.

The buggy came to a stop in front of the bank.

"Wait there," Mr. Hiott ordered the driver.

"Yessir," the servant replied, tipping his hat.

Mr. Hiott reached into his pocket and produced a set of keys. He unlocked the door, walked inside, and lit a lantern that was stationed near the entrance. "You don't have to do this," he said, turning to Rhett. "Taking the people's assets will only worsen their situation here. The war has already caused enough hardship."

A devious grin appeared on Rhett's face. "That's the plan, sir. I want the complete destruction of this city and its people. The war started here, so as I see it, the people in Charleston should suffer the most. Now, get moving."

They came to the vault. Rhett took the lantern from Mr. Hiott and held it close to the door for light. The vault was small, but secure. The door was made of heavy steel and secured by two locks which opened by key. Rhett had passed it many times, always wanting to look inside to see its contents. Now he had the chance. Mr. Hiott produced two keys from his pocket and unlocked both mechanisms. The door opened. He pushed Mr. Hiott out of the way and looked inside. The vault was nearly empty. He was shocked. There was no gold. Only a few small boxes containing silver coins remained, along with numerous stacks of Confederate bank notes.

"Where is it, old man?" Rhett asked angrily.

Mr. Hiott looked calm as he answered: "You were going steal the people's assets. But as you see, there are no assets left. This war has taken a financial toll on all of us—myself included. I have exchanged most of our gold and silver for Confederate notes. Our government needs finances to secure our freedom from your people. Gold and silver in the hands of our leaders provides them the means to buy guns, powder, food, and uniforms. Confederate paper money does us no good in the banks of England and France. So, as you see, this was a waste of time. You will not secure a better life for yourself by stealing from us."

Rhett was fuming. His plan for personal wealth was starting to unravel. "You're mistaken if you think I'm leaving empty-handed. I'm sure you have some gold stashed away for yourself. Take me to it."

He ignored Rhett's command. "Do you think you will make it out of here alive, Rhett? Do you really believe this grand plan will work?"

Rhett's fury became uncontained. He slapped Mr. Hiott hard across the face. The banker let out a whimper before falling to the ground. "I'm in charge here!" he screamed. "You will do what I say or I will...!" He stopped, not knowing what to say. Yet again, his temper bested him. He took a deep breath and calmed down. "Just give me what I want, and you and your daughter will live," he said, now in a softer tone.

Mr. Hiott stood up, wiped his face with his sleeve, and looked at his kidnapper. "My office," he said dejectedly.

"Then move," Rhett ordered, picking up the lantern and motioning Mr. Hiott down the hallway.

They walked to the last door on the right. Rhett turned for a moment, checking to see that no one had entered the bank while the two were at the vault. They were alone. Mr. Hiott unlocked his door and the two men went inside. Rhett put the lantern down on a table, illuminating the entire room. He then remembered something. It was rumored that Mr. Hiott kept a pistol in his desk drawer. "I've been told there is a Derringer in your desk. If you are thinking of using it, that would be a horrible mistake," Rhett advised him.

Mr. Hiott nodded an understanding before walking to a portrait on the far wall. It was an oil on canvas of George Washington in military uniform. Rhett watched as he pulled the corner of the portrait away. It swung away from the wall, opening like a door. Behind it was a safe. Mr. Hiott produced yet another key from his pocket and unlocked it. Rhett looked inside. There were small gold bars, maybe fifty in all, gleaming against his lantern's light. He was happy now. The angriness he felt about the empty vault was gone. "Sit over there," he told Mr. Hiott, pointing to a chair in the corner of the office. "Keep your hands on your knees."

Mr. Hiott complied.

Rhett began to pull the bars out of the safe. He put several in his coat pockets, but soon realized he needed a better way to carry the loot. He looked around to see a burlap bank bag sitting empty on the corner of the desk. He grabbed it and began to place the bars inside. Once full, almost too heavy to carry, he sat it back on the desk. "Come here," he ordered Mr. Hiott.

Mr. Hiott walked slowly over to his captor. "Are you satisfied now?" he asked sarcastically.

"Not yet," Rhett replied. He pulled his knife from behind his back and swung it at Mr. Hiott's head. Surprisingly, the banker was able to jump back, avoiding the slash. Rhett then charged at him, knocking him to the floor. He pulled the knife back for the killing blow, planning to drive the blade into Mr. Hiott's stomach. But again, he was thwarted. Mr. Hiott hit Rhett's arm, causing the blade to enter the left part of his abdomen, not his stomach. Mr. Hiott screamed in pain, grabbing his side. Rhett pulled his knife from the wound. A trickle of blood rolled off the blade and onto the floor. "You shouldn't have fought me," Rhett spat. "Your death would have been quick, but now you will suffer."

"Mr. Hiott!" a voice called out from inside the bank.

Rhett panicked. *How did they know I was here?* He put his knife back into the sheath and stepped back. Killing Calvin Hiott would have been a marvelous end to his evening, but he had to go. He grabbed the bag of gold from the desk and hastily exited the office. His destination was the rear door leading into the alley. Feeling for the door through the darkness, he turned the doorknob and pushed it open—he was out. He felt secure now, sure that he could slip away into the city streets. But before he could make it a few feet, he saw two men moving quickly down the alley in his direction.

"Stop there!" one of them yelled.

Rhett ran. He could hear men shouting. He ran faster, deeper into the alley that he knew led into one of the main streets. Then he heard a gunshot, two to be exact. Something hit him in his arm, something hard. The bag fell from his hand. Then pain. A warm stinging sensation made him cringe. He had been shot.

Chapter 27

Ellen was shoeless within a block, having discarded the footwear so she could move faster. Thomas was running as quickly as his bad knee would allow, but it seemed to be taking an eternity to get there.

"The one with the white door," Thomas said, pointing to a townhouse on the other side of the street. He needed assistance, realizing he couldn't go it alone. There was no time to fetch Lieutenant Chase. The barracks were too far from the bank. Help would have to come from his good friend John. He crossed the street quickly, Ellen holding tightly to his hand. He made it up the steps and knocked repeatedly. The door opened to reveal Inspector John James holding a candle in his nightclothes.

"Thomas? What's the meaning of this?" John asked, confused.

"I don't have time to explain, but I need you to come with me. We have to get to the bank as soon as possible."

John must have heard the distress in Thomas's voice, because he seemed to come alive instantly. "Come in, I'll get dressed."

Thomas and Ellen entered the home and watched John shuffle off. In less than two minutes he was back dressed in his usual attire, with a revolver hanging from his side. "Let's go," he said.

The three entered the street and began to run in the direction of the bank.

"We need to get there faster," Thomas said, realizing how much of a start LaCroix had on the trio.

John stopped abruptly and reached into his coat pocket. He pulled out a small shiny whistle and held it to his lips. With a large puff of air, the whistle producing a high-pitched sound. Nothing happened. Again, John blew the whistle. This time, the response was quick. The sound of hooves hitting the ground filled the night air.

John smiled. "Here comes my cavalry."

Two constables mounted on horses stopped in front of them. John ordered both off their mounts. He then took the reins of one and gave Thomas the other. "I've never seen you on a horse. Can you ride?" John asked.

Thomas could ride, there was no doubt about that. He just didn't want to. The fall that nearly killed him made him avoid the animal wherever possible. Tonight, however, he didn't have a choice. He swallowed hard. "Of, course I can. Can you?"

"Like the wind, son. Just try and keep up."

Thomas climbed on the horse and assisted Ellen up. She sat close behind him, wrapping her arms tightly around his body. "Hold on," he said.

"I will," she replied. "Just get there quickly."

John ordered the constables to meet him at the bank and to be bring any available men they could find.

Thomas thought about getting a message to Chase. It would be better if the lieutenant were there to help him. "Inspector, may one of these men deliver a message?"

"Yes, to whom?"

"Lieutenant Hudson Chase. He should be at the barracks by now. If there is any way to get a message to him informing him to meet me—?"

John cut him off, "It's done." He looked at one of the constables. "You men split up. Go get Lieutenant Chase from the barracks." To the other he said, "Meet me with reinforcements at the bank. Understood?"

Both officers replied in the affirmative before running off in different directions.

John snapped his horse's reins sending the animal galloping down the street. Thomas did the same but wasn't pushing his horse as fast as his friend.

In less than five minutes, they were there. Mr. Hiott's buggy and servant were outside the bank's front door. Both men dismounted and hitched their horses to a nearby post. Thomas helped Ellen down and walked her over to the buggy.

"Stay here until I call you inside," he told her.

She didn't object, but it was evident she wanted to go. A simple nod was her only reply. Samuel was off the buggy now helping Ellen into the seat. Thomas then turned to him. "How long have they been in there?"

"Not long, sir. Bout' ten minutes, I reckon."

"Alright. You stay with Miss Ellen."

"Yessir," Samuel replied, giving Thomas a curious look before a quick bow.

John was now at the front door of the bank, lantern in one hand, revolver in the other. Thomas pulled his gun as well. The urge burned inside him to use it on Rhett LaCroix, but he was better than that. The man had to be captured if possible. The public spectacle of hanging a Union spy would be good for the cause.

They opened the door cautiously and made their way inside. Although advanced in age, John moved in the manner of a much younger man. He was as stealthy as a cat stalking prey, moving from pillar to pillar for cover, cautious of the fact LaCroix could have obtained a gun.

They heard a yell from somewhere inside. Thomas yelled, "Mr. Hiott!" No answer. He and John moved into the hallway behind the teller windows, heading in the direction of the noise. Another yell, this one louder than the first. Traversing the darkness, they found Mr. Hiott on the floor of his office. John put the lantern down and knelt beside him. There was blood coming from his abdomen, and he was on the verge of losing consciousness.

"Where is he, Mr. Hiott?" Thomas asked.

"The back door, he's got a knife," Mr. Hiott replied in a low, labored voice.

Thomas didn't wait. He ran into the hallway. He made a right and followed the corridor to the end. There before him was an open door that led to the alley behind the bank. Quickly, he exited and took a right. It was a guess, really. He figured LaCroix would avoid the street, opting for the darkness of the numerous city alleyways. Behind him, coming up the alley, were two constables. Both were yelling at someone to stop. They must have seen LaCroix leaving, he quickly thought. Instinctively, Thomas lifted his revolver and fired a shot into the alley. He cocked the hammer and fired again. The constables stopped beside him, both men breathing heavily from their dash. "Hopefully one of those found the mark," he said to both of them.

The three men cautiously made their way to the end of the alley. Once there, Thomas felt deflated. The single alley split off in two different directions and LaCroix was nowhere to be seen. As he turned around to go back to the bank, he tripped on something, nearly losing his balance. He looked down to find a bank bag filled with small gold bars. Rhett LaCroix had gotten away, but he had done so empty-handed.

Back at the bank, Thomas entered Mr. Hiott's office. Two constables were lifting the banker off the floor in a gurney—he was still alive. Ellen was there now. She was crying while holding her father's hand.

Thomas put his arm around her in a comforting embrace. "He's going to be fine. They will get him to a doctor quickly.

"I hope so," she said. "Just promise me something, Thomas."

"Anything."

"Catch this horrible man. He has to be stopped."

Thomas pulled her close and kissed her forehead. "I'll catch him."

With those words of reassurance, Ellen left following the men who carried her father.

John looked concerned when he came into the room. He was wiping blood from his hands using a handkerchief. "It doesn't look good for him. He's lost a lot of blood."

"I know," Thomas replied. "Let's hope they can do something for him at the hospital."

"I believe it's time to enlist more help," John advised. "I've sent messages up the chain of command. We'll have every available man looking for him in a few hours."

"Where do you reckon he went?" Thomas asked, hoping the inspector's many years of police experience would allow him to provide a solid course of action.

"He probably wasn't expecting this tonight," John replied. "If he's planning to run, I bet he'll gather his belongings first."

"We should pay a visit to his room then?"

John nodded and put the red-stained handkerchief back in his pocket. "That'll be the best place to start. Think you can get word to your people on the north side of town? Make sure he doesn't get past the pickets?"

Thomas nodded. "I'll do it. No one will leave the city tonight."

"Good," John replied. "As long as he can't swim the harbor, he's got nowhere to go."

Chapter 28

His arm was bleeding, but the pain was manageable. Rhett had been moving so fast that he wasn't able to check the wound. He was lucky the bullet hadn't hit an artery. If it had, he would have already been dead. Going back to his room wasn't the wisest thing to do given what just happened, but he hadn't planned on this. He would need to gather his things and tend to his arm before getting out of the city. He put his key into the lock and opened the front door of the tailor shop. He hoped Mr. Brenton wasn't there. There wasn't anything, or anyone, that needed to slow him down. He found no one inside. The shop was dark. He moved speedily up the stairs and into his room. Using his good arm, he lit the candle on the table. He pulled off his jacket slowly, worried that the wound was worse than he thought. Rhett tore his shirt sleeve off and looked down. The bullet had only grazed his arm. A tight bandage would be all it required. He stripped the rest of his clothes off onto the floor. The good sleeve of his shirt was torn off and used to wrap the wound. Satisfied that the bandage would hold, he pushed his small bed out of the way, exposing the floorboards below. He pulled the loose board up and looked down. It was just as he'd left it. The revolver and ledger were lying on top of the folded gray uniform. As he removed the contents from the space, an exposed nail in the floor joist ripped a piece of the coat. It wasn't a major tear, just a bit of cloth torn off the sleeve.

In a few minutes, he was dressed in the uniform. He was amazed at how well he sized the major up that night in the tavern—it fit perfectly. Rhett secured the revolver in the holster and donned the light grey kepi cap. He was impressed at how professional he looked. No one would ever know he was a wolf in sheep's clothing. He would appear to be just another soldier doing his duty. He looked around the room for anything else he should bring. But there was nothing. No personal belongings, documents, and unfortunately, no gold. He had come to this city with nothing and would leave with nothing, except his pipe and his Bowie knife, both of which he tucked inside his coat. He opened the door and eased into the stairwell.

"What's happening here, Rhett?" Mr. Brenton's voice asked from behind him.

Rhett was startled. He hadn't seen the man standing there. The tailor was holding a half-used candle that illuminated his kind eyes. He appeared confused at the strange situation he had found at the top of his stairs. Rhett held out a calming hand before speaking, "Before you think anything, let me explain."

Mr. Brenton shifted the spectacles on the bridge of his nose. "I was hoping I was seeing things. But it seems I'm seeing everything clearly now," he said, shaking his head. "The men coming here were looking for you, it was no mistake. You in the uniform of a Confederate officer, well—"

Rhett cut him off, "There's no need to go any further." He liked the tailor. This was perhaps the one southern man he didn't want to kill, but he didn't need him running into the street yelling for help. This would surely make his situation worse than it already was. He only had a short time before the authorities showed up at his door anyway. "I don't want to have to hurt you, sir. I will admit that you've been very good to me during my stay here. For that reason, I'm going to give you the opportunity to let me pass without issue. If you don't, however; I'll be forced to take other measures."

Mr. Brenton didn't answer. He turned quickly and began to make his way down the stairs—he was going for help. Knowing he had no choice, Rhett pushed him forcefully from behind. The tailor left his feet and careened violently down the stairs, his body coming to rest in a crumpled heap at the bottom. Rhett descended the stairs and checked him for life, but there was nothing. Mr. Brenton was dead. He felt something deep inside him emerge at that moment. It was the one emotion he had not felt for some time, the one emotion he believed he had expelled from his soul—remorse. This now dead man had shown him kindness, and he had killed him in return. But he had no time for feelings. He was a professional. He had to move on. Stepping over the body, he walked out into the street.

Chapter 29

Thomas, Chase, and John were on horseback now. Chase had joined the men at the bank after Mr. Hiott had been sent to the hospital. They galloped to the tailor shop where LaCroix was living. The streets were far more desolate than usual. The sounds of the Yankee naval bombardment of Fort Wagner had made the citizenry nervous to come outside. The only people the men saw were a column of soldiers that moved through the street, pushed along by cursing officers who ordered them to march faster. They stopped just short of the tailor shop and dismounted.

"We need to move quickly once we're inside," Thomas ordered. He then turned to Chase. "Go to the back and make sure he doesn't slip out that way."

"Yes, sir," Chase responded, before scrambling off.

"Are you ready, John?" Thomas asked.

"Just ready to kill him if I get a good shot," John happily replied.

They entered the shop with guns drawn. Moving to the staircase where they planned to ascend the stairs to LaCroix's room, they stopped. A man was lying on the floor motionless. He was elderly, in his late sixties Thomas guessed. He bent down and felt for a pulse, but the man was dead. He remembered this man to be the shopkeeper who they spoke to yesterday. There were no stab wounds or bullet holes on the body, but it was clear the man's neck had been broken. *Keep going,* he thought. He and John stepped over the body and dashed up the stairs. At the top, Thomas stepped back and gave LaCroix's door a hefty kick with his good leg. Nothing happened. He knew the element of surprise was gone and hoped his prey wasn't waiting on the other side of the door with a pistol. He stepped back again, but there was a pause. He noticed his breathing was faster, heart pounding. It was the same feeling he experienced that day at Sharpsburg— the day he ran away from battle.

"Step back, son, let me have a try," John said, putting a hand on Thomas' shoulder. "I've kicked in one or two before."

Thomas didn't object. "Fine."

The old inspector took a pace back, and with a force Thomas didn't expect, he kicked the door off its hinges. Thomas raised the revolver and looked inside— LaCroix wasn't there. Only a single candle burned on the small table in the center of the room.

"Guess we just missed him," John said.

"Apparently so," Thomas agreed. "He must have killed the old man on his way out."

John moved back into the hallway. "If I don't need to stay up here with you, I'll go scare up some of my boys to help work this fella's murder."

"I'll be fine. Thank you, John."

John tipped his hat and descended the stairs.

Thomas stood there looking around the room. He hoped to find something, anything that could tell him what LaCroix's plans were. He saw the drawers were full of clothing and a suit was hanging by the bureau. He checked the pockets for any contents but only found some small shavings of tobacco. As he stepped back from the bureau, he tripped. He didn't fall, able to catch himself before crashing down. He took the candle from the table and illuminated the floor. A loose board protruding an inch or so above the rest snatched his attention. He reached down and pulled it up. There was, as he expected, an empty void. But examining it closer, he saw a rusted nail sticking out of one of the joists. On the nail was a piece of fabric—gray fabric. It's presence in the void was strange. There was no reason for it to be there. Thomas, Chase, and John hadn't thought to search in the floor yesterday when they were here. They had only looked in the bureau and under the mattress. Now everything was clear. He had been right about LaCroix being the suspect in the theft of the drunk major's uniform. LaCroix's plan was to escape the city in disguise. The uniform would allow him an exit—a safe and inconspicuous way out of Charleston. No sentry would question someone with the rank of major. Thomas heard someone enter the room. It was Chase. Thomas had forgotten about instructing him to watch the back stairs.

"Everything alright, sir?" Chase asked. "Inspector James told me there was no need for me down there anymore."

"He's right," Thomas said, standing up. "We missed him. But I think I've figured out how he plans to escape the city."

"How's that, sir?"

"I believe he's disguised himself as an infantry major," Thomas said, looking at the fabric in his hand. "He'll make it out if we don't do something quick."

The theory didn't seem to stir Chase into thought. He just looked eager to go hunting. "Where should we go now, sir?"

"John will need to stay here to work the murder of that tailor. You and I must get the word out to the sentries on the north side of town. Let's get to the horses."

Before the two men left the room, Thomas looked around again. He hadn't paid it much attention at first, but a financial ledger lay closed on the room's table. Not sure if its contents had anything to do with LaCroix's plans, he picked it up and placed it under his arm.

The two men made their way out of the room and down the stairs. They were met by John and a group of constables who were carrying the body of the tailor out into a wagon. "You need any help, John?" Thomas asked.

"We've got it from here. What are your plans for LaCroix?"

Before Thomas could answer, the sound of cannon fire filled the night. All the men turned and looked toward the harbor.

"I've never heard a barrage quite like that," Chase remarked. "Must be readying an infantry assault."

Thomas forgot to answer John's question, as his mind began to put the pieces together. The death of the courier who carried orders about Fort Wagner's armaments and the theft of the uniform made him realize that LaCroix's mission was to help the Yankees capture the fort. The importance of Wagner to the harbor's fortifications was no secret. The Yankees had already launched one assault trying to capture it. The timing of his attempted bank robbery also provided solid information as to his plans. Thomas knew LaCroix wouldn't have done it this evening if he had planned to spend more time in the city. He looked over at John who was still waiting on a reply. "My plan is to look for him within our ranks, John. I think our man will try to get into Fort Wagner. I believe he intends to meet his comrades there when the fight is over."

"What do we do now?" John asked.

Thomas looked toward the harbor. "I'll go to Wagner."

John stared at him before answering. "Just be careful. It sounds like it's heating up down there."

"I will," Thomas replied, remembering the ledger under his arm. He handed it to John. "Take this and give it a look, if you don't mind."

John patted Thomas on his arm. "We'll look at it together after LaCroix is caught. Won't we?"

Thomas appreciated his optimism. "Yes, we will."

Chapter 30

Rhett couldn't help but feel good about his work. Except for getting shot in the arm and losing the bag of gold, everything had gone to plan. *Well, maybe not*, he thought. He had left Colonel Marlow's financial ledger in his room. Too focused on the uniform, taking the book slipped his mind. It was a mistake he wished he wouldn't have made. The information within its pages would have surely pleased his superiors. But now wasn't the time to worry about his mistakes. He had to focus. The most difficult part of his mission was yet to come. He was needing to gain entrance to Fort Wagner and set a charge that would blow the fort's powder magazine.

Approaching the wharf, he noticed the harbor was hot with activity. Exploding shells and flares lit up the night sky, illuminating the boats that carried soldiers to defend various posts. Rhett pushed his way past the line of enlisted men waiting to be ferried. There, he found a young lieutenant peering out into the water.

"Lieutenant!" Rhett shouted.

The officer turned quickly. He looked at Rhett's collar and noticed the single star. He came to attention and saluted. "Yes, Major?"

"I must be taken to Morris Island at once. I have important orders to meet with the commander there."

"Yes, sir." The lieutenant dropped his salute and looked down at a document in his hand. An older sergeant, who Rhett could tell was standing as a sentry, held a lantern close so that the lieutenant could read. "Your unit, Major?"

Rhett didn't think he would be asked any questions. He assumed the orders of a Major would be powerful enough to garner him passage. "Unit?" he replied loudly. "I'm telling you that I need to deliver orders, son!" He knew yelling may help get his point across, but then decided it wasn't wise to cause a scene. He stepped a little closer to the officer and softened his tone. "I can only tell you this is a confidential matter, Lieutenant. I am needing to make it there as soon as possible. This is extremely important to the defense of this city."

The lieutenant looked nervous. He finally motioned for Rhett to walk to the lower dock. "Right this way, sir. That dispatch boat can get you to the island."

Rhett nodded and made his way to the lower dock. Waiting there was a small row boat with two soldiers standing by on the oars.

"Take the major to Morris Island," the young lieutenant called down to them.

Rhett was pleased at how easy that was. But he knew there would be more difficulties to come. He hadn't forged any orders allowing him into the fort. He hoped he would be able to talk his way inside there as well.

Rhett stepped into the boat and took a seat. The two soldiers pushed off from the dock and began to row. The sound of the cannon fire coming from the harbor entrance was becoming more frequent. He knew this meant the attack was coming soon. He had to be in the fort before the infantry made their assault. To detonate the magazine after the attack would do no good. "Put your backs into it, boys!" he ordered the soldiers. The soldiers complied, rowing faster.

After a few minutes, he saw a small side-wheeled cotton clad approaching from the distance. The two soldiers began to row closer to the shore so the vessel could pass.

"That's the *Gov'nor Pickens,* sir," one of the soldiers said. "She's the one carryin' the boys back and forth to the fightin'."

Rhett didn't care. "Just focus on the oars, boy. I don't need any conversation."

"Yessir," the soldier replied.

It took nearly an hour for the boat to make it to Morris Island. The soldiers tied up to the dock located between Battery Gregg and Fort Wagner, letting Rhett off. He stepped onto the shore and looked over at the battered Confederate bastion. The fire being poured into the fort by his navy was steady and severe. The Union ships illuminated the fort using flares, allowing Rhett to see just how badly it had been bombarded. He cautiously walked up the causeway toward the fort's rear gate. He knew it would be suspicious for an officer to ask to gain entrance without any orders, but he hoped that the fort's defenders would be too distressed to ask any questions.

The beach sand was not easy to traverse. Coupled with the fact he had hit the ground twice for incoming shells, it took longer than he expected to make it to the gate. Once there, he found a sergeant and two privates standing guard. The sergeant saluted him before holding out his hand. "Orders please, sir."

Rhett hoped to lie his way inside, just as he did on the wharf earlier. "My orders are to help in the fort's defense, Sergeant. Now, allow me through."

The soldier shook his head before speaking. "Major, sir, I'm supposed to check—"

Rhett walked close to the soldier and put his hand on his shoulder. "There is an army of Yankees just down the beach. Now, I'm here to help make sure they don't capture this fort and kill each and every one of us. It'll be in your best interest to let me inside and waste no more of my time. General Beauregard himself gave me verbal instructions to deliver to the commander here." The sergeant's eyes were wide now. Rhett hoped the mention of the general's name would be enough to allow his entry. Beauregard was the commander of all Confederate forces in the state, and he was highly regarded by most men under his command.

"I'm sorry, Major. Please enter, sir," the sergeant said.

Rhett strolled past the three soldiers triumphantly. The scene he encountered inside was nothing short of chaotic. The steady barrage of cannon fire had laid waste to much of the structure. Men were running, officers shouting, and dead bodies were strewn everywhere. But this was good for him. The chaos of battle would shield his movement to the powder magazine. He stayed close to the inner walls, attempting to find his target, but it was too dark to see anything clearly. The only light provided were the short flare bursts as they crossed over the top of the fort. Then he saw it: a palmetto log enclosure just on the other side of the parade ground. Covered by a double layer of sandbags, he assumed this was the magazine. He crouched down behind a low wall needing to think. He hadn't planned on what to do after making it inside. The powder magazine was his objective, but he wasn't sure how to take it. He realized there would be a soldier inside acting as a guard.

He also knew he couldn't shoot his way in. The sparks from his revolver could ignite the powder inside, sending the magazine, and himself, exploding skyward. Rhett would have to talk his way in. So far, his gift of persuasion had served him well.

He began to walk across the parade ground toward his objective. But just before making it there, an eerie silence fell over the fort. The cannon fire stopped. He walked back to the wall and again crouched down. This was what he didn't want to happen. Although dangerous for him, the cannon fire from the navy kept the soldiers inside the bombproof and out of his way. Within minutes, he heard shouting. Officers yelling at sergeants, sergeants yelling at the enlisted men. The bombproof door opened and out they came carrying muskets, swords, and grenades. The gray clad soldiers looked hungry for a fight. They ran through the parade ground and up onto the parapet, moving quickly, mostly in bare feet. Rhett was surprised at how high their spirits were, assuming that the naval barrage would have lessened their will to fight. He glanced to his left to see an officer approaching him holding a lantern. His heart raced knowing he hadn't yet formulated a story. Rhett turned his back to the approaching man hoping he would pass by.

"You!" the officer yelled.

Rhett turned around slowly. He could see the officer was a captain, who now saw the star on his collar. Rhett could see blood on the captain's coat, as if he had been assisting with some injured men.

"Oh, I'm sorry, Major," the captain said embarrassingly. He then saluted Rhett and stood at attention.

Rhett returned the salute. "Can I help you, Captain?"

"No, sir. I was ordered to find some able-bodied men to assist in getting the wounded to the rear. I didn't realize you were a major. I'll be on my way, sir."

Rhett saw an opportunity here. He could move freely about the fort helping move the wounded. He would only have to keep up the charade for a short time until the inevitable infantry assault. There would be enough activity then to make his move.

"Wait, Captain," Rhett said, stopping the officer who was already walking away. "I'll assist you the best I can."

The captain smiled. "Thank you, sir. Right this way."

He was led by the captain to the bombproof shelter located just under the parapet. It, like the magazine, was constructed of palmetto logs and topped with sandbags. Once inside, he was immediately struck by the odor of death that filled the small space. Several men were already on gurneys ready for transport and several others were dead. His attention was drawn to a surgeon standing over a screaming soldier. The doctor was pulling a bone saw from his kit, preparing for an on-site amputation.

"Will you help me carry this one out, sir?" the captain inquired, pointing to a soldier lying on the ground.

Rhett answered, "I believe I will be better at directing the effort. You and one of those privates get this one out. I will go and try to recruit some additional men for the effort."

"Yes, sir," the captain replied.

Rhett stopped the captain before he and the private picked up the soldier on the gurney. "And what was your name, Captain?"

"Fields, sir. Timothy Fields."

"Very good, on your way now."

The captain and private lifted the wounded soldier and carried him away. Rhett waited a moment before exiting. He saw the gray soldiers running back and forth, climbing the parapet, preparing their muskets. He knew he would have to wait to take any action until the Union assault was at its peak. So, he waited, and he watched. The right time would surely present itself. And when it did, he would singlehandedly destroy Fort Wagner and all the Rebels within.

Chapter 31

Thomas and Chase pushed their way through the crowd of soldiers to the end of the wharf. Thomas had no orders allowing him passage, and the lieutenant in charge of allowing men on the steamer seemed immediately irritated at the request.

"I'm sorry, sir," the lieutenant apologized, "but there is no one allowed on board without the proper orders."

"Listen to me, Lieutenant," Thomas said, trying not to sound too harsh. "I'm in pursuit of a Union spy that we believe is on his way to Fort Wagner."

The lieutenant shook his head. "I'm just following orders, Captain. I've been ordered to only allow personnel with the proper orders onboard."

Thomas looked over at the docked steamer. Its name was painted in red lettering on the side, *Governor Pickens.* Some three dozen cotton bales lined the sides of the vessel, acting as a makeshift barrier from any incoming Yankee shells.

Thomas couldn't give up, not when he was so close. He knew there was no overland route that could get him to Morris Island. He tried another approach. "Have you allowed any other officer passage without orders tonight?"

"Well, sir," the lieutenant said nervously, not finishing his reply.

"Answer me, Lieutenant!"

"Yes, sir, but only one."

"Was he a major?"

"Yes, Captain, he was a major."

Thomas moved in closer. "Was he a little taller than me? Black mustache?"

"Yes, sir. That's him."

"Then I must tell you that you've made a horrendous mistake." Thomas paused for a moment and shook his head. It seemed LaCroix's disguise was working. "What is your name, Lieutenant?"

"Please, sir. I have already been disciplined earlier this month. I don't need any more trouble," the lieutenant explained, almost in a whisper.

"Your name, Lieutenant," Thomas demanded.

"Trapier, sir. Louis Trapier."

"That man was a spy, Trapier. He stole a major's uniform so he could get into Wagner. I'm not supposed to be telling you this, but I want you to understand how important it is that I'm allowed on board."

The steamer's whistle blew loudly as a company of men scrambled on board. The ship was readying to leave.

The lieutenant nodded. "Right this way, sir," he said, gesturing toward the gangplank.

As Thomas and Chase walked by the officer, the lieutenant grabbed Thomas's sleeve and stopped him. "I'm sorry, Captain. His story seemed believable."

Thomas patted the lieutenant on the shoulder but didn't reply. He really didn't know what to say. The man had been fooled by a trained spy. But in fact, many people had been fooled by LaCroix in the past week. This man fared the same as everyone else.

Thomas and Chase crossed the gangplank onto the steamer. They were surrounded by enlisted men from a Georgia regiment. They were mostly silent. The distant cannon fire was growing more rapid now, and Thomas was sure the sounds added to the men's already fragile nerves.

The steamer's whistle blew again, alerting the dock workers to untie the mooring lines. Within a few minutes, the vessel was making its way out into the harbor.

"It doesn't look good over there, sir," Chase observed.

Thomas turned and looked at the island. Chase was right, it didn't look good. Artillery shells being fired from the Yankee ships seemed to light up the night sky. Although too far off still to see the fort, Thomas could imagine the scene. It would be hell on earth, and he felt sympathy for the men who were fighting inside.

"You're right," Thomas answered. "Let's just hope we catch up to LaCroix before he makes matters worse."

"What do you think he intends to do, Captain?"

Thomas wished John were here now to help him answer that question. He had been invaluable so far, but civilians weren't allowed anywhere near the fighting.

"I don't know, Chase," Thomas replied. "I really don't know."

The nervousness was evident in Thomas's young aide. The man had never seen combat. In truth, Thomas was nervous too. Although trying to suppress the anxious feelings he had when confronted with danger, they had returned when he tried to kick in LaCroix's door. John had to intervene then, finishing the task. He hoped if the time came to be courageous tonight, he wouldn't shy away from danger. It would be the only way to gain back his self-respect.

"May I tell you something, sir?" Chase asked, staring into the harbor.

"Yes, Lieutenant."

"I feel responsible for some of what's happened. If I would have captured him that night at the Jones house, some people may still be alive."

Before Thomas could provide any reassuring words, the whistle of an incoming shell was heard in the air. With nowhere to run, all the men hit the deck. Seconds later—an explosion. The steamer had been hit.

The jolt sent both men flying. Luckily, they landed close to a rail. They held on tightly as the steamer, now on fire, began to list severely to one side. The screams of the soldiers who were injured by the explosion filled the air. Thomas looked in the water to see many of the men who were thrown from the ship bob up and down before slipping beneath the dark water of the bay. He was powerless to help them. It was a scene worse than he ever imagined.

"What are we going to do, sir?" Chase shouted.

"Hang on to the rail until the boat hits the bottom!" Thomas yelled back. "Can you swim?"

"Yes, sir, like a fish!"

The forward half of the *Governor Pickens* was now completely submerged, and fire was steadily consuming the rest of the ship.

"Start swimming in that direction when we get in the water!" Thomas ordered, pointing to the edge of the harbor. "And kick your boots off! There'll be no need for those!"

After a few minutes, the boat began to roll over on its side. Thomas gave Chase the nod. Both men used their one free hand to pull off their boots and remove their hats. Releasing their grips simultaneously, they slid down the deck and into the water. They swam together a short way before bumping into a floating barrel. Thomas and Chase clung onto it, using it as a makeshift lifeboat.

"Kick!" Thomas shouted.

They paddled themselves over to the beach just below the fort. Crawling onto the shore, they lie on their backs for a moment, tired from their struggle.

"What now, sir?" Chase asked, sitting up, still trying to catch his breath.

Thomas turned and looked at Wagner. The navy had slowed their fire, which meant the infantry assault was soon to follow. "We need to get there as quickly as possible. No stopping."

The two men made it to their feet and began across the sand. The absence of their boots turned out to be a blessing, because they were able to make better time without them. The loss of Thomas's revolver was not a blessing, however. He reached down on his side to find it missing, realizing it was now on the bottom of Charleston Harbor.

The two made it to the rear gate. There was no one outside. The eerie absence of soldiers meant the enemy attack was coming. Every available man would be ordered inside to defend the walls. Thomas yelled up toward the parapet, "Hello!"

"Who goes there?" a voice called down.

"Captain Altman with the provost marshal!"

There was silence. Both men waited for a response.

"Captain," Chase said, breaking the silence. "I want to ask you something."

Thomas felt an uneasiness in his voice. He looked over at the young man who appeared as wet and uncomfortable as he did. "Yes, Lieutenant?"

"If something should happen to me, will you tell my father I was a brave soldier?"

Thomas knew Chase's rattled nerves had caused him to ask the question. He tried to provide some reassuring words. "We're going to be fine. We just have to keep our wits about us and remember what we came here to do."

"Yes, sir," Chase answered, not sounding convinced. "But just in case something does, will you tell him?"

Thomas knew Chase had never seen battle. The job in the provost marshal's office was a safe one, nowhere near the fields of death. But Thomas didn't need his young comrade in a negative frame of mind. Chase needed to focus now. "You mustn't think like this," Thomas said. "You've more than proven your bravery the night LaCroix tried to kill you. Trust me when I say that you're a brave man, no matter what happens tonight."

Chase dropped his head. "Sorry, sir. There's a lot to think about right now."

Thomas put his hand on Chase's shoulder. "I know. I feel the same way."

The door beside the rear gate opened and a captain walked out. His face was dirty, his uniform bloodstained. Two soldiers stood behind him with muskets at the ready.

"What are your orders?" the captain asked.

"I'm tracking a spy who I believe to be inside the fort," Thomas replied.

The captain walked up to the two men and looked them up and down. Thomas knew they were a mess: no shoes, uniform wet, covered in sand.

"Come in," the captain said, wearily. "If indeed there's a spy in here, he's come at a bad time."

The captain offered Thomas a handshake. "Timothy Fields."

Thomas shook his hand. "Thomas Altman. What's the situation now?"

"The Yankees are forming down the beach outside of artillery range. All men are at their posts waiting for them. The colonel said we aren't retreating— fighting to the death if we have to," the captain said, taking his hat off to wipe some sweat from his dirty forehead. "Now what were your saying about a spy?"

"The man I'm looking for is disguised as an infantry major. He has a mustache, black hair, a little taller than me."

A look of recognition appeared on Fields's face. "I just met a major who matches that description. He's offered to assist us with moving the wounded."

"Can you take us to him?" Thomas asked.

"I'll try," Fields answered, before pointing at Thomas's empty gun holster. "Better find yourself a pistol, though. You may need it shortly."

Chapter 32

      The time had come to make his move. Rhett needed to get to the powder magazine, set the charge, and get out of the fort without raising any suspicions. The fort's artillery had begun to fire on the Union infantry. Rhett knew that meant his comrades were making their way up the beach. He pulled the revolver from his holster and carried it low in his right hand as he made his way across the empty parade ground in the center of the fort. The powder magazine was in sight now. He happened to glance to his right. He saw the one thing he didn't want to see: Captain Thomas Altman. Quickly, he ran over to the steps leading up to the parapet. Fury was the only emotion he could feel now, enraged that his plans had somehow been found out by this increasingly resilient man. He ran onto the parapet where he tried to keep an eye on Altman, all the while trying to appear as if he belonged there. He saw that his two pursuers were accompanied by the captain he had already spoken to, Fields. The sound of musket fire from just in front of the fort redirected his attention. He didn't know what to do. He walked to the edge of the wall where a regiment of soldiers were crouched down waiting for the Union troops to get closer. To assist in fighting his own men would be wrong. But to act as though he wasn't going to fight would be worse.

"Ready!" an officer a few feet away from him yelled.

The troops stood up and aimed their muskets over the wall. Rhett pushed his way to the front of the line, aiming his already drawn pistol into the darkness. A young private beside him glanced at him for a moment with a curious look. He realized the men around him would wonder who he was, but hopefully the flying bullets would direct their attention elsewhere.

"Fire!" the officer ordered.

The muskets fired in unison. The sound shook the ground beneath Rhett's feet. He fired his revolver at the same time, intentionally aiming high so as not to hit his friends on the beach.

"Reload!" was the next order called.

Rhett backed up now, trying to appear that he was remaining in the fight, without being in the fight. He looked down into the parade ground but didn't see Altman. This worried him. *What if he finds me up here? There will be nowhere to hide then.* He realized his only option would be to fight his way out, killing any man who tried to stand in his way.

Small arms fire was striking the side of the fort. He didn't want to be killed by fire from his own troops; he knew he didn't need to step back into the firing line. To try and make it to the powder magazine with his pursuer somewhere about the fort was also dangerous. Head down, pondering what move to make, a hand landed firmly on his shoulder. Nervously, and slowly, he turned around.

"Major, are you in this regiment?" a colonel asked, appearing indifferent to the bullets that whizzed above his head.

Stiffening, Rhett placed his revolver in its holster to appear non-threatening. "No, sir," was all he could say.

"Then you are who these men must be after," the colonel said, sidestepping to reveal Captain Altman and his lieutenant standing there. Before Rhett could react, the two men were on him. They each grabbed an arm while the colonel removed Rhett's revolver from his holster.

"Been looking all over for you, LaCroix," Altman said. "Now, let's go have a talk."

Rhett stared down at the ground. He wanted to seem aloof, not paying attention to the leather bindings being applied to his wrists by the lieutenant. They were holding his arms together tightly; there was no way he could wiggle out. Realizing there was nothing left to do but play the part of the defeated enemy, he would remain quiet and formulate a plan of escape.

As he was moved down the steps of the parapet by the two men, he could hear the battle growing severe. *They'll be over the wall soon,* he thought to himself.

Chapter 33

Thomas felt victorious after the arrest. LaCroix had murdered at least three people, if not more, and was now being led to the bombproof of Fort Wagner. It was a job well done in his mind, but he knew he had been lucky as well. The captain who let him inside the fort's walls told him about a major he had never seen before assisting with the injured men. Thomas then proceeded from regiment to regiment asking their commanders if they had encountered any officers whom they didn't recognize. A colonel of Georgia troops was quick to point out LaCroix, who Thomas found lurking in the rear of the firing line. Surprisingly, the arrest went well. LaCroix was so surprised in fact, he didn't have the chance to attempt an escape.

The three men, Thomas, Chase, and LaCroix, entered the bombproof after being allowed entry by a young corporal guarding the entrance. It was dark inside. Three lanterns hanging from hooks on the wall did a poor job illuminating the space. It did, however, provide just enough light for Thomas to see LaCroix grinning broadly as Chase sat him on an empty ammunition crate.

"I wouldn't be smiling if I were you," Thomas suggested. "I'm sure you know you will hang as a spy in the morning."

LaCroix turned to Thomas, the grin smaller now, but still there. "I'm not smiling at what you believe my fate to be, Altman. I was simply amused by your sad appearance."

Thomas and Chase were still wet, still shoeless. They looked affright.

Chase spoke up, "You will die soon knowing you were bested by us. It appears you were not ready for such a pursuit."

"I believe I will be the victor when all this is over, Lieutenant," LaCroix mused. "It won't be long until my comrades make it over that wall. And when they do, I will watch as they bayonet you both to death."

Although Thomas knew LaCroix was trying to goad them, he realized the spy had a point. If the Yankees captured the fort, LaCroix would surely be freed, and both he and Chase would surely be killed. He quietly thought for a moment about his options. Should he stay, or should he try and make it back to the city? Could he even make it back now? He went with his gut feeling. "Chase, keep an eye on him while I check the situation outside. We need to get him back tonight and lock him up in the city jail."

"Yes, sir," Chase replied.

Thomas moved in close to LaCroix and looked sharply into his eyes. "Don't try anything."

"I would never," LaCroix replied. "But before you go, just one thing."

"And what's that?"

"I want you to know that when I do make it back to my people, I will begin planning Ellen Hiott's death. You won't be alive to protect her, so I want you to know now how she will die."

Without warning, Chase slapped LaCroix hard in the face—so hard that the spy's mouth filled with blood. He spat some on the ground before saying, "Never mind, Captain. I can see your friend doesn't want to listen. A pity though; in my mind, I would find it pleasing. Piece by piece I would cut her apart."

Chase raised his hand to hit LaCroix again, but Thomas grabbed his arm in mid-swing. "That's enough. He's not worth the energy."

"Sorry, sir," Chase replied, before taking a calming breath.

Thomas released Chase's arm and patted him on the shoulder before exiting the bombproof. As he entered the parade ground, he saw the fight on the parapet becoming severe. Men were firing one after the other, some were falling dead. Seeing this brought forth a familiar feeling: fear. He hadn't felt it while looking for LaCroix. He was too focused on his objective to allow his mind to think on it.

"Captain!"

Thomas turned to see Captain Fields running up to him.

"We need your help up top!" Fields shouted. "We need to plug a hole in the line!"

Thomas swallowed hard. "I have to get back with the prisoner!" he yelled back.

"Please, we need help!" Fields shouted back.

Thomas was nervous, scared in fact. But he realized this could be his redeeming act. His cowardly behavior at the Battle of Sharpsburg could finally be atoned for. He knew that today could be the day he proved to himself that he was not a coward.

He nodded a response to the captain. He knew that would be enough.

Fields led him up the steps onto the parapet. Thomas clutched the revolver he had taken from LaCroix tightly in his right hand. He was led to a spot just behind a low wall that faced the beach. A company of battered soldiers stood there at the ready, prepared to fight the blue hoard that was now marching toward the fort.

"Right here!" Fields shouted, pointing to a space beside a dead officer. The man was lying on his back, eyes still open, face covered with blood. Thomas stared at the body for a moment, hoping he would avoid the same fate.

Thomas took his place while Fields left to fetch other personnel. He looked out onto the beach. The glow of the flares bursting overhead provided a view of what was coming. Hundreds of Yankee soldiers were now marching in the fort's direction. He cocked the hammer back on the revolver and waited. Just then, the company beside him leveled their muskets and fired a volley toward the enemy. Thomas looked onto the beach after the smoke cleared. The bullets had not slowed their progress. They kept coming. It seemed quick after that. Closer now, twenty yards, ten—now they were climbing the wall. He fired a round at the first blue uniform who stepped over. He fell. More were coming over. Again, he fired. He hit another man. The fear was now giving way to excitement. He hadn't fled; he held his ground. He felt like a warrior now. He aimed at another Yankee just coming over the wall. He pulled the trigger, but the revolver clicked; it didn't fire. The soldier ran toward him with the butt of his musket raised. Thomas threw his hand up to block the incoming blow, but he wasn't quick enough. The butt struck him on the right side of his head. The pain was horrific. He felt as if his skull had been crushed. Then blackness. Then nothing. His motionless body fell to the sandy ground. The battle continued to rage around him.

Chapter 34

The sounds of the battle echoed through the small bombproof. Rhett was still sitting on the ammunition crate, hands tied behind his back. He noticed the young lieutenant was getting antsy, pacing back and forth. His captor was much younger than he. Given this, Rhett felt he may be able to sway this rebel into making a mistake. Although he truly believed the Union regiments would seize the fort, he felt his odds of survival greatly improved if he could make it out by himself. It was time to use his gift of persuasion yet again. "Lieutenant, these straps are hurting my wrists," he said, trying to appear uncomfortable, fidgeting on the crate.

The lieutenant turned to him with a less than concerned look on his face. "Things are as they should be. You aren't entitled to any comforts."

The sound of musket fire was growing rapidly. Rhett could tell the battle was almost at full swing. He watched as the lieutenant walked to the bombproof door, trying to listen to what was happening outside.

"I can't go anywhere, you know," Rhett said, smiling. "It would be better to help your captain than to watch me. After all, there is a guard on the other side of the door, is there not?"

The lieutenant looked back at him. His facial expression was different than before. Rhett could tell he had struck a chord.

"Just sit there," the lieutenant spat back. "I don't need your opinion."

At that moment, an explosion outside rocked the bombproof. Rhett fell off the crate and the lieutenant fell to the ground. Rhett pulled himself up and sat on the sandy floor, his ears now ringing from the sound. The lieutenant appeared equally as dazed, having to use the wall to assist himself to his feet.

"That was close," Rhett said concernedly, hoping the lieutenant was unnerved by the shell.

The lieutenant walked over to Rhett and thrust a finger into his face. "You stay in this bombproof and make no attempt to escape. The guard will be ordered to kill you if that door opens."

Rhett didn't smile this time. He dropped his head. "Yes, sir."

The lieutenant turned quickly and left, closing the bombproof door behind him.

Rhett wasted no time. Reaching his bound hands up behind his uniform coat, he pulled the Bowie knife from his waistband. He couldn't believe they didn't check him for weapons. Had they done so, Rhett wouldn't have had this opportunity. Quickly, and with precision, he used the knife to cut through the straps. Free now, he stood up and walked to the door. It would be foolish, he knew, not to heed the lieutenant's warning about the guard. To open the door and attempt an escape would surely lead to him being shot. He would have to get the guard to enter somehow, then incapacitate him. Acting on this thought, he knocked loudly on the door. The sound of his fist pounding the wood was muffled by the sounds of musket fire outside. He pounded again. Nothing. He had to escape the bombproof, but there was no other way out. Unless it was opened, he was stuck here. Feeling helpless, he leaned up against the wall. Rhett was concerned this was to be his last moment of quasi-freedom. The last time he would be somewhere besides a prison cell. But then the door opened. In walked the guard holding a lantern.

"What is it?" the guard asked.

The guard was a young man of no more than twenty years. His hands were shaking and he appeared frightened. It was obvious to Rhett he was concerned about the blue invaders pounding away at the fort's walls, and he hoped the boy would be too worried about the fight outside to consider a bound captive was in any position to kill him. So, he made his move. The guard wasn't given any time to put up a defense before Rhett lunged forward with a closed fist. The guard tried to level his bayonet at the incoming threat, but he was far too slow. The blow landed squarely on the soldier's face, sending him quickly to the hard, sandy ground. *Too easy,* Rhett thought. He picked up the unconscious guard's musket and took several percussion caps and a handful of cartridges from the guard's ammunition pouch.

Rhett opened the bombproof door and looked outside. The scene was as he had anticipated. Soldiers running from one direction to the other, officers shouting orders, injured men being carried to safety. To his dismay; however, the Union soldiers had not yet fought their way inside. Slowly, he exited the bombproof into the parade ground where he loaded the musket. But Rhett didn't know where to go now. He looked over at the rear gate, which was now closed. Several soldiers stood close to it, at the ready should any attackers break it down. He was in a tight spot. The only way out, he now reasoned, was over the parapet, in the direction of the Union Army. This was risky. To make his way between the forces would be sure suicide. If not killed by an enemy bullet, a friendly one could easily do the same. There was another option, however, albeit an equally dangerous one. To blow the powder magazine as he first intended would make the fort susceptible, maybe even cause a hole large enough for the troops to enter. This, Rhett realized, was his only option.

As he began toward the magazine, a loud volley of musket fire was heard on the parapet, followed by the sound of clashing metal. Rhett looked up to see the Union soldiers making their way inside. The idea of now blowing up the powder magazine was out. To do so would be to risk killing his own men. He lowered the musket to the ground momentarily and stripped off the uniform coat. He was now clad in a white shirt, stained with the blood from his wounded arm. Although not in a blue uniform, he hoped the difference in his appearance might help him from being killed by his own people. Picking up the musket, he now moved calmly over to the parapet steps. He would fight his way out.

Chapter 35

"Captain!" was what Thomas heard. "Captain, sir!" It was louder this time.

Opening his eyes, he found Lieutenant Chase crouched beside him. He had a splitting headache, coupled with blurred vision. He couldn't remember why he was on his back and in so much pain.

"Up sir, you must get up!" Chase cried. "The Yankees have made it inside!"

Thomas struggled to his feet, assisted by Chase. He steadied himself against a wall, waiting for his vision to clear. Once so, he looked to his left to see his comrades trying to push the invaders from the fort. The fighting had now become hand-to-hand combat. It was a hellish scene.

"Sir, your revolver!" Chase said, handing Thomas the weapon.

He opened it and checked the cylinder—only two balls left. That would have to be enough for the moment. He would pick his targets wisely. "Move toward the breach, Lieutenant! We have to push them back onto the beach!" he yelled to Chase.

Chase smiled, showing his enthusiasm. "Yes, sir!"

But before the two men could make their way over to the outer wall, Thomas remembered LaCroix. He grabbed the lieutenant's arm stopping him. "Where's the prisoner?"

"Under guard in the bombproof, sir!" Chase shouted over the gunfire.

"Very well!" Thomas replied, looking over to the parapet steps. He was satisfied with this answer, but only momentarily. Illuminated by the fires that were now burning throughout the fort, he was easy to spot—it was LaCroix. The spy was brandishing a musket, clad in a white under shirt, moving to where the Yankee soldiers had breached the wall. Thomas didn't wait. He ran as fast as his legs could carry him. Chase, looking confused at this sudden burst of speed, followed close behind. As they made it closer, Thomas noticed the enemy soldiers retreating back over the wall. They seemed to be leaving as quickly as they had come. The yells and huzzahs of the Confederate troops filled his ears as he made his way to where he had seen LaCroix last, but once there, the spy was gone. He had vanished into the mass of soldiers who were now preparing to defend another enemy assault.

"Where did he go, sir?" Chase asked nervously.

Thomas didn't know. LaCroix could have gone over the wall or he could be hiding inside.

The Yankee artillery began to fire at the fort once again. This was a clear sign of their intentions. A quick pounding of the fort's walls would prelude another infantry attack. The soldiers began to file in line, preparing to move into the fort's bombproofs until the barrage was over. Thomas and Chase didn't move though. They looked at the soldiers as they passed, hoping LaCroix was trying to hide amongst them. But this proved fruitless. Thomas then looked over the parapet wall onto the beach. Seeing only a mass of dead and mangled bodies, his spy was not there. He sighed with frustration. He couldn't believe all his hard work had been in vain.

This one man who had caused so much destruction made it back to the safety of the Yankee lines.

Another shell landed nearby. The explosion sent several dead bodies, along with a considerable amount of sand, flying into the air. Thomas looked around to find they were the only men left on the parapet. Every other soldier in the fort had retreated to the bombproofs. Although wanting to stay and look for LaCroix, he had to go. He grabbed Chase by the arm. "We need to move out."

As they were readying to leave, Thomas saw a shadowy figure moving up quickly behind Chase. Without warning, Chase's body jolted forward, and his hands flew into the air. Thomas reached in and pulled Chase toward him, but the young lieutenant's body fell motionless to the ground. It was all happening too fast for Thomas to see what was coming next. The force of something hard struck him on his bad knee. The blow sent him careening to the ground. The pain he felt shoot through his body was immense. He let out an agonizing scream. He was unable to think, unable to move. His revolver had fallen out of his hand on the way down. He was utterly helpless now. No weapon, no one to help him. He opened his eyes and looked up. Into the dim light appeared Rhett LaCroix. He stood over Thomas smiling, holding a musket in his right hand, a knife in the left.

"You were wrong to leave me alive, Altman," he said. "It was an easy task to overpower a lone guard. Especially a rebel one."

Thomas paid the comment no attention. He was only concerned now with Chase. He turned his head and looked over at the lieutenant. He wasn't moving.

"Your friend is dead," LaCroix said. "I plunged the knife deep enough to pierce his heart."

The whistle of an incoming shell made both men look skyward. Perhaps it was divine intervention, perhaps sheer luck, but this gave Thomas a chance. He kicked LaCroix in the lower leg, sweeping his feet from under him. As the spy fell, the shell struck the fort. The explosion was massive. Fire flew from the level below, sending a shockwave down the parapet. Thomas struggled to his feet hoping to jump on LaCroix. But the spy was faster than he was. LaCroix stood up and ran to the outer wall. Thomas was trying to keep up, but his knee was slowing him down. He watched as LaCroix jumped over the wall and rolled down the embankment into the ditch below. The musket he was carrying fell from his hands. As soon as the spy hit the ditch, he was up again, stumbling toward the enemy lines. Instinctively, and forgetting about the pain, Thomas stepped over the wall in pursuit. He, like LaCroix, was unable to handle the steepness of the sand fort's façade. He rolled uncontrollably into the ditch, landing a few feet from his now waiting enemy.

"You won't give up, will you?" LaCroix shouted.

Thomas, not responding, realized he was yet again in a bad spot. He had no gun, no sword, and no knife. He was being driven completely by emotion, unable to consider the dangerous situation he had put himself into by pursuing this man.

LaCroix pulled a knife from behind his back. "The courier I killed begged for his life before I killed him!" he said, looking at the blade. "But you won't be given the chance to beg!"

Thomas, sitting in the knee-deep water of the ditch felt something under him. He reached down for it as LaCroix approached. It was a bayonet, freed from the end of a musket. He gripped it tightly and brought it a few inches from the top of the water.

LaCroix lunged fast. The blood-stained knife came from high behind his head. Thomas raised the bayonet from the murky water quickly, trying to stab LaCroix on his way down. But LaCroix parried the blow, knocking the bayonet from Thomas's hand. LaCroix was bringing the knife back up for the killing blow, when Thomas heard a gunshot. It was close, he realized...very close. LaCroix's eyes opened wide, his mouth fell open. It was a look of confusion and bewilderment. He dropped the knife and fell to his knees, then face down into the ditch. Thomas couldn't believe what had just happened. He crawled over to LaCroix and checked him for life; he was dead. Rhett LaCroix had been shot in the back. He looked up to see Chase, a few feet away, on his knees. Thomas lifted himself from the ditch and ran to him.

"Chase! Are you alright!" Thomas yelled, kneeling beside him. He thought Chase was dead, and yet, here he was. The lieutenant was covered in blood and his breathing was labored. A revolver lay just inches from his hand. Chase had shot LaCroix.

"Sir, please," Chase said, his voice barely a whisper.

"Let's get you into the fort! We need to get you to the surgeon!" Thomas yelled, trying to lift Chase from the ground.

"No," Chase replied, again quietly, pulling Thomas down. "Please promise me you will tell my father I died like a soldier. Tell him I died a hero."

Chase realized he wasn't going to make it. This was his last request. "I'll tell him, Lieutenant. I'll tell him."

Chase looked at Thomas a moment before taking one last breath.

Thomas sat there for a moment motionless, holding the body of his aide, his friend, the man who had saved his life. He tried to fight back the tears, but it was no use. He cried, he screamed, he asked God why. It was, by far, the worst moment of his life.

The artillery fire slowed now, which meant the infantry attack was getting ready to begin. His knee felt weak and nearly shattered from LaCroix's blow, and he knew he couldn't get Chase's body up the hill to the fort. Releasing his deceased friend, he limped up the sandy embankment to the wall.

Once inside, Thomas fell to the ground. He felt horrible, physically and mentally. He could barely walk, had a splitting headache, and his closest confidant had just died in his arms. This was war, he thought. It was hell. As he sat there stoically, a distressed sergeant came up to him.

"We need some help, Captain," the sergeant said. "Our lieutenant was hit, sir. We have no one to command the company."

Thomas turned slowly and looked at the soldier. There was no giving up now. Chase's life would not be given in vain. He knew how he had to respond. "Fetch me a revolver and show me to your position. We'll fight until the last man if we have to."

Chapter 36

It was hard for Thomas to write, but he had made a promise to Chase. It was the most important letter he would ever pen. He pulled the paper out of the top drawer of his desk and sat it in front of him. Before beginning, he told himself to let the words flow naturally. He wrote:

Sir,

I have been advised by our adjutant that word of your son's death has already reached you. Words cannot describe how sorry I am for your loss. Not being a father myself, I have no way of knowing the pain you must be going through. I know my attempts at consolation may not offer you any form of comfort, but I would like you to know how important Hudson Chase was to me and to his country.

I believe it is important for a father to know how his son died. I do this to dispel any rumors which might find their way to you, thus clouding the truth of his story. He died as a result of a knife wound delivered by a Union spy. This spy had devices to blow up Fort Wagner, which would have allowed a Union assault force to capture Morris Island. The wound did not immediately cause his death, as he was able to kill the spy shortly before the villain was able to end my life.

I would also like to tell you how important it was to him that you know of his bravery. His dying wish was for you to know how valiant he was on the field of battle, and how he met his end fighting the enemies of his country. For if not for the bravery he showed that night, I would not be able to write to you now. Your son saved my life, and for that, I am eternally grateful.

In closing, I hope and pray that you and your family will be able cope with this tragedy. Lieutenant Chase was a brave man who unselfishly gave his life for others, and I, for one, am glad he possessed this wonderful trait. Should I be of any service to you or your family during this trying time, please do not hesitate to call upon me.

Your obedient servant,

Captain Thomas Altman

He sat back in this chair and put his pen down. He hoped this letter would offer something besides sadness to an already sullen affair. He would have willingly given his life that night to save the lieutenant's. But that wasn't what happened. He would have to live with the events as they transpired.

One of Thomas's new aides, Lieutenant Telfair, entered the office without knocking. "Captain, sorry to bother you, sir," he said, snapping a salute. "Inspector James is here to see you."

"Show him in, Lieutenant."

Telfair walked away and John entered.

"Good afternoon, young Thomas," John greeted happily. He sat down and put a financial ledger on Thomas's desk. It was the same one that Thomas removed from LaCroix's room. John nodded toward the book. "There's more than a fair share of interesting things in there."

Thomas was curious to know what. "Tell me about it."

John leaned forward in the chair and tapped the cover of the ledger. "It seems Colonel Marlow was making a great deal of money selling seized cotton," John explained. "I can only guess this had something to do with his untimely death."

"You're saying he was abusing his power?" Thomas asked.

"Ha!" John laughed. "I would say it was more than abuse. The man even made money from the enemy. Yankees were buying the cotton through the lines, according to this. That's called treason in my book."

"I wouldn't have guessed that," Thomas admitted.

"There's more," John said. He reached into his pocket and pulled out a pipe—LaCroix's pipe. "Look familiar?" he asked.

Thomas's eyes widened. "Where did you get this?"

"It was in the pocket of Rhett LaCroix. Turns out I know the sergeant who oversaw the digging of the graves out there. He pulled it off him before they buried the body."

Thomas felt vindicated. He was right that the killer of Colonel Marlow was LaCroix. The presence of the pipe in the spy's pocket proved this. He also realized the possession of the ledger by LaCroix meant that he was, in fact, Marlow's bookkeeper. All the pieces now fell into place.

John stood up and put his hat on. "I'll leave you the ledger to look over. Going to be a lot of people in trouble after all this is revealed," he said. "Oh, and you can keep the pipe too. I thought it would be a nice keepsake."

Thomas was at a loss for words. "Thank you, John," was all he could muster.

"That's my job," John replied. "I just wish I could have killed him. I've wanted to bag me a Yankee since the war started."

Thomas grinned. He had heard this from his friend before. "Maybe you'll get the chance. The war isn't over yet."

"Maybe," John answered. "Have a good evening."

"You too."

Three hours passed. Thomas didn't anticipate being here this late—8 o'clock. Going through Marlow's ledger made him lose track of time. Its pages were full of information implicating Confederate officials in selling or receiving stolen cotton. He was eager to report his findings, but it would have to wait until tomorrow.

As he put on his gloves to leave the office, Lieutenant Telfair appeared in his doorway. His new aide was sweating profusely, as if he had been running. Telfair had been relieved from duty three hours ago, which made Thomas wonder what he was doing here now.

Telfair saluted before pulling a piece of paper from his pocket. "Sorry, sir," he began, "but I forgot to give you this message earlier. It was left for you here around noon. I didn't remember I had it until I reached the barracks."

"Its fine, Lieutenant," Thomas replied, taking the message. "You're dismissed."

The Lieutenant beat a hasty exit while Thomas unfolded the small piece of paper. It read:

Bring the ledger. Follow the map and come alone. Disobey me and she dies.

LaCroix

He dropped the note on the desk, horrified. Rhett LaCroix was dead. Why was his name written here, he wondered? Question after question ran through his mind. Again, he looked at it. Turning it over, he found a sloppily drawn map showing a location somewhere north of the city. Then he looked at the writing again. He focused on two words: *she dies.* That could be only one person. He ran from his office to his horse outside, the ledger tucked under his arm. Mounting up, he put the book into a saddle bag, before kicking the animal into a run.

Five minutes later, he was there. He leaped from the horse and ran to the door. The servant, Samuel, threw the door open before he could knock.

"Is Ellen here?" Thomas asked frantically.

A look of concern was easily visible upon his face. "She ain't here, sir. Ain't been back since her walk this morning. That ain't like her, Captain."

Thomas's heart dropped into his stomach. He stood there furious at what was transpiring, and equally confused at what was going on. He moved closer to the servant. "There has to be something else. Did she say where she was going? What time did she leave?" He felt his temper flare. "Just give me something!" he shouted, now inches from the servant's face.

Samuel closed the door and walked onto the steps. He looked to be near tears now, lifting his right hand to produce a small piece of paper. "A man come by, Captain. Said you would be by looking for Miss Ellen. He told me to give this to you but not to tell nobody else. The man said he kill me if I didn't do what he said."

Thomas took the note and read it:

Come alone.

Simple, two words, nothing else. He crumpled the paper and put it in his pocket. But before he made his way down the steps, he stopped and turned back to the servant. "Bring me a paper and a pen and do it quickly."

Chapter 37

       Thomas arrived at a small, unimpressive, cabin just off the bank of the Cooper River. It looked abandoned, but the map led him to this spot. He had worried about her the entire journey. Ellen had been brought into a situation she should have never been a part of. But why? Someone must have known he loved her, for there would have been no reason to do this. And the ledger. What secrets did it hold that were so important? He tried to calm his mind, reason logically. It was impossible though. The name, *LaCroix,* written at the bottom of the note defied logic. The man was dead. Hudson Chase had seen to that. So here he was, hiding behind a cypress tree, confused and nervous. The cabin was just a few yards away.

       The door opened. Thomas looked around the tree to see a man exit holding a lantern. He was large in stature, thick as a tree trunk. "I heard your horse, Captain," the man said in a deep voice, talking into the darkness. "Come inside with the ledger but leave your pistol on the porch. Any trickery will cause both of you to lose your lives." The man then went back inside and left the door open.

       Both of you? The comment confused him. Ellen must be inside, he thought. Taking a deep breath, he stepped into the clearing in front of the house. He had no choice but to follow instructions. Anything he did otherwise would jeopardize Ellen's safety. Thomas pulled his pistol out of the holster and dropped it on the porch floor. He felt vulnerable doing so, but his sword was still on his side. The man said nothing about it.

Thomas entered the shack to find the man sitting at a table. He didn't recognize him. The stranger had a long scar that ran down the entire length of this face and wore a rough green riding jacket.

Thomas raised his left arm slightly to show the ledger tucked underneath.

"Good," the man replied, devoid of emotion. "Have a seat."

Thomas sat down in the chair across from the stranger and placed the ledger on the table. "Where is she?" he asked calmly.

The man shrugged. "I'll show you."

Standing up, he moved a door behind him. He opened it to reveal Ellen, noose around her neck, standing on a shifty crate. She was conscious, gagged. Her eyes opened wide at the sight of Thomas.

"Ellen!" Thomas shouted.

"Sit!" the stranger yelled back, closing the door. Thomas reached for his sword, but the man pulled a gun. He pointed it at Thomas. "Move your hand from the blade, Captain," he ordered. "I'll kill you before you even have the chance to draw it."

Thomas knew he was right. He did as he was told. He sat down and gestured to the ledger. "This is what you wanted. Let her go."

The stranger returned to his seat, his pistol still trained on Thomas. "First, allow me to introduce myself and explain my reason for our meeting," he began. "My name is Hawkins. I was an associate of Rhett LaCroix. I signed his name to the note only for amusement. He is, as

I'm sure you know, still dead. Had he been a better spy, however, he wouldn't have lost his life that night at Wagner. I, on the other hand, believe in winning, not losing. As you can clearly see, I have gained the upper hand here, something my colleague failed to do." Hawkins stopped for a moment to take a drink out of a pewter cup before continuing. "I learned about this ledger through one of my informants. It contains information that would destroy the careers of some of our high-ranking officers. I've been tasked by one of these aforementioned officers to retrieve it. He wants his career to remain untarnished."

Thomas cleared his throat. "Thank you for the explanation," he said stoically, "but all I require is to leave here with the girl."

Hawkins shook his head. "Sorry, Captain. Although I thought earlier about letting both of you live, I've changed my mind. To let you leave would be to allow you to track down more of our spies. Which, I must say, you have a talent for doing."

A rush of fear overcame Thomas. He couldn't believe what was happening. The worst part was that Ellen would die too. But he wouldn't go out without a fight. He couldn't die knowing he tried nothing to save them both.

Hawkins pulled the hammer back on the pistol and grinned. Thomas knew he had to make his move. He put his hands up in a motion of surrender and pushed his chair back slightly. Quickly, he lifted his good leg and kicked the table as hard as he could. The table flew across the floor toward Hawkins, striking the man squarely in the chest. This knocked him to the ground, but the pistol remained in his hand. Thomas drew his sword and pulled the blade back. There was no chance to aim the strike. He only hoped for good results. And he got them. His sword sliced into Hawkins's arm. A shrill scream was his enemy's reaction followed by him dropping the gun to the floor. Thomas kicked the pistol away while watching the man grab his arm, writhing in pain. Instinctively and without thinking, Thomas delivered a kick that landed on the left side of the spy's face. Hawkins was knocked unconscious from the blow. *Ellen,* Thomas thought. Running to the room she was in, he pushed open the door. Her eyes again widened at his sight, but this sudden excitement forced her to lose concentration on her footing. She stepped off the crate and the noose tightened around her neck. Thomas raised his sword and cut the rope away from the ceiling, just before it tightened, saving her life. He lowered her to the floor.

Thomas pulled the gag from her mouth. "Are you alright?" he asked.

"Yes," she answered simply, holding him tight.

"Thomas!" Ellen suddenly screamed, pointing behind him.

Hawkins was standing a few feet away at the door. He was holding his bleeding arm tight to his body, while his uninjured arm displayed his pistol. Thomas wished he had picked the pistol up instead of just kicking it away, but saving Ellen was the only thing he could think of at the moment.

Hawkins pointed the gun at them. There was nothing he could do now. He and Ellen stared at each other, both knowing what was going to happen. If he had to die, he was happy it would be in her arms. He had proven he was no coward, found the love he had been missing, and helped save his city from invasion. Had he lived past tonight, it would be a great beginning to the rest of his life.

Thomas and Ellen put their foreheads together and closed their eyes. The gun fired. Thomas cringed. He heard something hit the floor. He opened his eyes and turned around. Hawkins was on the floor dead. The gun in his hand hadn't been fired. Cautiously and confusedly, he and Ellen rose to their feet. That's when Thomas saw him. It was John. His friend stood behind the body of Hawkins holding a smoking revolver.

"I would have been here earlier if your map had been better drawn," John said.

Thomas let out a sigh of relief. He wasn't dead, Ellen was safe, and a Yankee spy was lying on the ground deceased. It was hard for him to believe this strange turn of events. John James had just saved both of their lives. "I'm glad to see you, John," he said.

John holstered the revolver and smiled. "Had the servant not fetched me, this could have turned out rather bad, wouldn't you say?"

"Agreed," Thomas replied.

John stood over Hawkins's body and prodded it with his boot. "I've wanted to kill myself a Yankee since the war started."

Thomas patted John on the shoulder. "The chance to do so couldn't have come at a better time."

Chapter 38

It was the following morning at the Hiott house. Thomas saluted the general and stood at attention.

"No need for that, Altman," Ripley said, half-saluting back. "We're both here as friends of the family today, not officers of the Confederacy."

"Thank you, sir."

"I wanted to tell you personally how much I appreciated your work," the general said. "Had it not been for you, Wagner may have been taken."

"Lieutenant Hudson Chase was the real hero, sir. I'd like that noted in the official report."

Ripley looked down for a moment and shook his head. "There won't be any *official* report, Captain. We can't allow the enemy to know just how close the spy came to his objective. We want them to believe we knew about their plan all along. Do you understand?"

"Yes, sir."

"Good," Ripley said. "I also appreciate the information you've found in Marlow's ledger. It will be put to good use, I can assure you."

"Thank you, sir."

Ripley and his entourage left the house. Thomas made his way down the hallway and into a large bedroom. Lying on the bed covered with a white sheet was Mr. Hiott. He had lived through the assault by Rhett LaCroix. Beside him was Ellen. She turned to Thomas as he entered the room.

"Father is feeling much better today," she said with a smile.

Thomas walked up to her and held both of her hands. "That's good. How are you feeling?"

It had only been two days since Thomas and Ellen's near-death experience at the hands of the spy, Hawkins. He was concerned the event may take its toll on her, causing mental anguish.

Ellen pulled Thomas in close. "As long as you are with me, I'm fine." The two stared into each other's eyes a moment before sharing a kiss.

"Ellen," Thomas heard Mr. Hiott say, causing them to suspend their show of affection. They walked over to the bedside where he was awake now, trying to sit up.

"Father, Thomas is here," Ellen told him softly.

"I see," he replied, nearly in a whisper. "I would like to apologize to him."

Thomas moved closer. "There's no need for apologies, sir. I only wish you to recover from your wounds."

"Nonsense, Captain. I realize I acted harshly toward you. I'm embarrassed about having been deceived by that rascal, LaCroix." Mr. Hiott coughed. His body convulsed in pain.

"Please, Mr. Hiott, try to rest. I give you my word that we may discuss this later."

Mr. Hiott nodded and turned his head. Thomas stepped back and watched as Ellen laid a wet cloth on his forehead. Once Mr. Hiott was back asleep, she reached for Thomas's hand and led him out of the bedroom.

"Do the doctors think he will fully recover?" Thomas inquired.

"They do, and I hope they're right."

"You mustn't worry," Thomas instructed. "You will become unwell yourself."

Ellen smiled and pulled him to the back door. "Shall we walk?"

"There is nothing that would make me happier," he answered.

The two walked out of the house and into the garden. But as they began their stroll, cannon fire was heard in the distance. The guns of Fort Sumter had acquired a Yankee target. Thomas knew the city's defenses would come alive to repel the threat.

"Do you have to leave?" Ellen asked. She looked disappointed at the forthcoming answer.

It had been a week since Thomas had almost lost his life at Fort Wagner, and two days since his encounter with Hawkins. These events had made him reflect upon the more important things in life. He used to believe regaining his honor as a soldier was paramount to anything else. But he realized he had been wrong. Life was what he appreciated most, and he intended to make the best of it from now on.

"No," he answered. "The cannons have already interrupted one of our walks. I intend to finish this one."

The End

Made in the USA
Columbia, SC
28 August 2024

41235877R00115